Front picture, King Æthelstan,
(or how I visualised he might have looked in the year 925)
Æthelstan was described as a handsome beautiful boy,
and according to his wife Alan has sustained those
attributes.

I am thankful to Alan Cook for allowing me to use his
picture on the front cover of this novel -
'The Forgotten King.'

The Forgotten King

The Forgotten King

By
Robbie Cottrell

Poem from the Saxon Chronicles "Battle of Brunamburh"

*Never, before this, were more men in this island
slain by the sword's edge,
as books and aged sages confirm,
since Angles and Saxons sailed here from the east,
sought the Britons over the wide seas,
since those warsmiths hammered the Welsh,
and earls, eager for glory, overran the land.*

Æthelstan

894/5 - 939

I have deliberately used the term
'Saxon'
as opposed to 'Anglo-Saxon'.
It is highly debatable if the name
'Anglo-Saxon'
was ever used during the period of
Alfred and Æthelstan.

Stories that claim to be "based on a true story" mix fiction with nonfiction by taking an event or events that happened in real life and changing certain details. This differs from historical fiction. In historical fiction the plot is original, but the settings and/or characters are based on real life.

Other books by Robbie Cottrell

Factual book

Thomas Doggett Coat & Badge (300 years plus of history)

Fiction books

*****

Mister Doggett

The Tide Waiter

The Arsonist

The Clergyman

The Flag

A Pinch of Salt

*****

Meet the author
Robert (Robbie) Cottrell

With special thanks to Toni Mount, Ian Nicholson,
Ray Hudson and John Crawford

PARKINSON'S^{UK}
CHANGE ATTITUDES.
FIND A CURE.
JOIN US.

Special thanks to the staff of King's College Hospital, London.

9

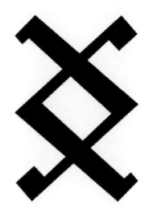

In the year 924 Æthelstan became the king of all the Saxon peoples and, in effect, the first King of all Britain.

Saxon Months of the Year

January - *Aetera Geola, translates as the month after Yuletide.*

February - *Solmonath, derived from wet sand or mud. According to Bede it meant the month of cakes.*

March - *Hredmonath, honouring an ancient (but little known) Anglo-Saxon fertility goddess named Hreoa or Rheda.*

April - *corresponds to Eostremonath or the pagan deity relating to the Spring Equinox.*

May - *Thrimilce, the month of three milkings when livestock were so often well fed on fresh spring grass, they had to be milked three times a day.*

June/July - *were jointly known as Lioa meaning mild and gentle. June was referred to as before-mild, and July as after-mild.*

August - *was Weodmonath, or the plant month.*

September - *Waligmonath, meaning the Holy month when we celebrate a successful summer's crop.*

October - *Winterfylleth or the winter full moon. Winter was said to begin on the first full moon in October.*

November - *Blotmonath, or the month of blood sacrifices, probably because this was the month when older infirmed livestock that might not survive through the winter months were butchered as a food stockpile.*

December - *Aerrala, meaning the month before Yule.*

The use of the Anglo-Saxon Germanic calendar dwindled as Christianity was introduced more widely across England in the early middle Ages. It brought with it the Roman Julian calendar which quickly became the standard so that, by the time Bede was writing, he dismissed the Germanic calendar as 'the by-product of olden times.

When the Germanic-speaking peoples of Western Europe adopted the seven-day week, which was probably in the early centuries of the Christian era, they named their days after those of their own gods who were closest in attributes and character to the Roman deities.

It was one of those peoples, the Anglo-Saxons, that brought their gods and language (what would become English) to the British Isles during the fifth and sixth centuries AD.

In English, Saturday, Sunday and Monday are named for Saturn, the sun and moon respectively, following the Latin.

The remaining four days (Tuesday, Wednesday, Thursday and Friday) are named after gods that the Anglo-Saxons probably worshipped before they migrated to England and during the short time before they converted to Christianity after that.

Tuesday is named for the god Tiw, about whom relatively little is known. Tiw was probably associated with warfare, just like the Roman god Mars.

Wednesday is named for the god Woden, who is paralleled with the Roman god Mercury, probably because both gods shared attributes of eloquence, the ability to travel, and the guardianship of the dead.

Thursday is Thunor's day, or, to give the word its Old English form, Thunresdæg 'the day of Thunder'. This sits beside the Latin dies Iovis, the day of Jove or Jupiter. Both of these gods, like Thor have been associated with thunder in their respective mythologies.

You may recognise a similarity here with the name of the famous Norse god Thor. This may be more than coincidence. Vikings arrived in England in the ninth century, bringing their own very similar gods with them. Anglo-Saxons were already Christian by this time but may have recognised the similarity between the name of their ancestors' deity Thunor and the Norse god. We simply don't know, but the word Thor does appear in written texts from the period.

Friday is the only weekday named for a female deity, Frig, who is hardly mentioned anywhere else in early English. The name does appear, however, as a common noun meaning 'love or affection' in poetry. That is why Frig was chosen to pair with the Roman deity Venus, who was likewise associated with love and sex, and was commemorated in the Latin name for Friday.

It was Ray Hudson who first planted the seed of Æthelstan into my head. The longer I researched the history of this great man I understood how he must, at first, have lived under the shadow of his grandfather - King Alfred. However he finally moved out of the shadows to prove to the Saxon nation that he was his own man. He took his grandfather's dreams one step further, namely to unite the Saxon race into what eventually became England, derived from the Old English name Englaland, which means 'Land of the Angles'. The Angles were one of the Germanic tribes that settled in Great Britain during the Early Middle Ages.

The Anglo-Saxon dynasty was relatively short-lived, starting around 450 when the Romans left and ending in 1066 with the Norman Invasion of William the Bastard.

The Saxon brothers, Hengist and Horsa, led a massive attack in 455. They marched from Thanet through Faversham to Canterbury and eventually arrived at Aylesford, which is near Maidstone, where a fierce battle took place. Following the death of Horsa, the surviving brother Hengist ruled as King of Kent. He reigned for 33 years and died in 488. He was succeeded by his son, Oeric Oisc. The kings of Kent, known as Oiscingas, traced their descent to Hengist through Oisc, who was eventually succeeded by his son Octa.

Prologue

Maeldunesburh

Wiltunscir

My name is Alder, first born son of Alander, and I am twelve years old. When my father died, my mother took me to the Abbey for educational training. I am left-handed so the monks called me the 'evil one,' from the Latin word 'sinistra.' I considered myself bright, and despite my arrogance Bishop Aldhelm took me under his wing. The Bishop employed me as one of his scribes at the nearby Abbey of Maeldunesburh, working under his supervision, but that was before I became our future King's chosen solitary scribe. I think he had heard the rumours about me and wanted to check if I was evil or not.

The locals informed me that Bishop Aldhelm was a Saxon by birth and closely related to the Kings of Wessex. He became the first Abbot of Maeldunesburh Abbey, and his royal connections gave him a certain amount of control over the surrounding villages. Aldhelm also had close connections with His Holiness the Pope which saw the Abbey being placed under papal jurisdiction. This was, of course, a high honour.

Later Aldhelm became Bishop of Scireburnan, the former capital of Wessex. He had an ever-increasing diocese that extended throughout much of Wessex and the south-west of Britain including Wiltunscir, Sumorsaete, Durnovaria, Dumnonia and West Wealas. The latter is extremely misleading as it was swallowed up by the neighbouring kingdom of Dumnonia. It still feels strange to recall the land as Englaland, as prior to

Æthelstan's reign we only had the seven Heptarchy. That was a time when Wessex and Mercia were all powerful, a time when the kingdom of West Saxon and their kings extended their rule over most of southern Britain. That is, after all, the true meaning of Wessex - West Seaxna.

As an individual, Aldhelm was well respected and genuinely cherished by his parishioners. Tales evolved about Aldhelm playing music which attracted large crowds and he often told stories regarding the life of Jesus. He was well educated, speaking both Greek and Latin. It is also said that he was a highly skilled architect, as well as being a great scholar and technician. After Æthelstan's death he was recognised as building the first organ in Englaland in Maeldunesburh Abbey.

Æthelstan was born a bastard in Wessex in the year 894/5, the base born son of Edward and his consort Egwina. He became the first king of all Englaland and the first monarch to introduce a common currency, and silver coins were imprinted with his portrait. He was knighted at an early age and given a sword with a golden scabbard as a sign of his high rank and authority. Throughout his life he showed genuine affection towards Maeldunesburh, especially to those men who fought alongside him in battle. As a result, he created the 'Commoners of Kings Heath' or the 'Old Corporation'. This honour continues to pass down through their freemen descendents to this very day.

King Æthelstan told his advisors of his yearning to be buried within the confines of Maeldunesburh Abbey.

Æthelstan proved to be an effective king and was aware that stringent laws should be made for specific crimes which I will speak of later. He introduced 'shrievalty' which appointed shire reeves, or sheriffs, to act as important officials to oversee the shire or county. Æthelstan increased his powerbase by marrying his sisters to influential European kingdoms, with the precious jewels and sacred relics from their dowries often being kept in Maeldunesburh Abbey.

Æthelstan first suggested I should work with him as his chronicler to ensure a true untarnished history of his ancestors, including his grandfather King Alfred and his son. His purpose in life was to guarantee a factual bloodline that would never be lost to time or bastardised by his enemies.

Past chroniclers tended to deliberately remove or simply choose to forget certain events from our history, doubtless because it would bring back unpleasant memories of the past. However, a battle lost, or an earldom's assassination should always be faithfully recorded. Æthelstan was constantly intrigued by the suggestion of a second coming which he surmised to be at the turn of the new century. It tantalised him, not through vanity but the chance to meet face to face with the son of God, either in heaven or on earth, and to confess his sins to Jesus himself rather than Bishop Aldhelm.

His father, Edward, an ætheling prince of the royal house of Wessex, was the natural successor to his grandfather's throne. Bishop Aldhelm, like many of the high nobles, knew that Alfred favoured my father as his rightful successor to the throne. It was only when Alfred's advisors suggested the king should be known as 'The Great' that his orders, and that of my father should never be criticised. Alfred never considered himself as 'Great' and steadfastly refused to be ever associated with that name.

When his father Edward succeeded the throne, he had to defeat a challenge from his cousin Æthelwold, who considered himself as having a stronger claim to the position. He attempted to raise an army to support his claim but was unable to get enough support to meet my father in battle. Æthelwold eventually fled to Viking-controlled Northanhymbre, where they accepted him as a king. In later years he sailed with a small fleet to Bemfleot in Essex, where the East Saxons also accepted him as a king.

This type of challenge was commonplace throughout the seven kingdoms when a monarch had recently died.

Æthelstan's, half-brother, Ælfweard, inherited the throne upon their father's death. However, Ælfweard died within two weeks of his ascension on the seventeenth day of Aeferaliva 924. Æthelstan was immediately cleared of any collusion in Ælfweard's death and in the following year crowned King of Wessex. Edward and Ælfweard were buried alongside each other at New Minister in Venta Caester.

So it was that the unprepared Æthelstan inherited the empty throne of Wessex upon Ælfweard's untimely death. Out of curiosity I checked the various scrolls appertaining to Ælfweard's death and found nothing out of the ordinary to indicate murder or treason.

As time passed by, I became extremely close to Æthelstan. He was a likeable and peaceful man, pious and devout, tall with fair hair and skin, handsome and beautiful. He was an attractive man who the ladies adored, and they swarmed around him like bees about the honey pot. Strangely he never married, despite continuous advice from the Witan for the need for an heir to the kingdom of Wessex. Æthelstan maintained his sole purpose in life was to follow in his grandfather's footsteps by bringing the seven Saxon kingdoms closer together and create the Kingdom of Englaland, although I wondered how this might be achievable without the shedding of blood.

His other passion was putting quill to parchment to produce an honest history of what he hoped would be the coming together of the great seven Heptarchy. He had six siblings, one of whom eventually ascended the throne after his death but Æthelstan was always the favoured son. Unfortunately, he rightly surmised that, following his death, the kingdom and everything that Alfred, Edward and he had fought for all their lives might be lost to disloyal kinsmen or foreign invaders. Cousins were always scheming. The Vikings forever set their envious eyes on Nordhymbralond, East Anglia, Sussex and Essex, whilst the Irish and the Welsh had similar ideas about Mercia, Dumnonia and the far-western shires of Britain. North of the Roman wall, the Celts and Picts constantly carried out raids across the border to steal our cattle and make slaves out of our peasant farmers.

One day when Æthelstan was in an exceptionally bad mood, he vented his feelings out on me. He stated rather forcibly that, 'This land is Englaland! It will never be Daneland!' He apologised soon after, which was his way, full of fury one minute and subtle the next. 'Please accept my sincere apologies. I do not feel myself today.'

I knew the crown weighed heavily on his mind. He was particularly anxious of what the future might hold for Englaland.

'No apology needed, Sire. You clearly have much to think about, for being a King cannot be easy.'

Æthelstan obverse and reverse silver penny

Chapter 1

In The Beginning

Those sinful creatures had no
fill of rejoicing that they consumed me,
assembled at feast at the sea bottom.
Rather, in the morning, wounded by blades
they lay up on the shore, put to sleep by swords,
so that never after did they hinder sailors
in their course on the sea.
The light came from the east,
the bright beacon of God.

'Shall we commence the chronicle today, Sire?' I asked this question with a slight tremble in my voice, and carefully kept my eyes from his as I softly asked another. 'Have you decided where we should start?'

'Probably best to start with my earliest memories of the time of Alfred and those, with whom he surrounded himself,' he said. 'After acceding to the throne, Alfred spent several years fighting Viking invaders, and he won a decisive victory at the Battle of Ethandun. The village lay under the northern slope of Salisbury Plain where that great monument to our ancestors was erected. Following Alfred's success, he made an agreement with the Vikings to create what we know as the Danelaw in Northanhymbre, which is north of the tidal and turbid Humbre and south of Monkceaster and the Tinan. Alfred also oversaw the conversion of the Viking leader Guthrum to Christianity, but I will speak in depth on this subject later. He defended his kingdom against the Viking attempt of total conquest, and from becoming the dominant ruler in Saxon Britain.'

There was a long pause, during which I looked up at Æthelstan. He met my gaze and looked particularly serious, and I wondered what he was going to say next.

'Before we start this chronicle, I will tell you one thing, and you will promise me never to speak of it again. There is no truth in the burning of the cakes story. That was a private jest between my grandparents, but unfortunately some people took it literally. This deeply upset him, but the silly joke might have taken place in the month of February which would explain much.

'I am constantly asked about grandfather and why we all considered him 'Great'. He refused to accept the title during his lifetime, for it was more of a nickname, just like his Saxon name which meant 'wise-elf' or 'elf counsel.' Perhaps in the future other generations will remember him as 'great', but not ours.

'I only knew my grandfather for about five years before he succumbed to a mystery sickness of the gut. I remember him being an avid reader and tactician, but most of all I remember his agonising facial expressions. His stomach always caused him considerable distress. His pain was greatest after performing his morning ablutions, but as a young boy I never knew if that was the cause of his death.

'Alfred had a reputation as a learned and merciful man of a gracious and level-headed nature, and he always encouraged education. Grandfather was hardly mentioned during the short reigns of his older siblings Æthelbald and Æthelberht.

The Saxon Chronicles of the time describe the Great Heathen Army of Norsemen, landed in the kingdom of Ēast Engla Rīc, becoming the place of the East Angle settlers. Their intention was to conquer every Saxon kingdom which made up Saxon Britain.

'Alfred's public life began at the age of sixteen with the accession to the throne of Wessex by his third brother - Æthelred. During this period, Bishop Asser gave Alfred the unique title of secundarius, which indicated a position similar to the Celtic tanist, and as a recognised successor closely associated with the reigning monarch. This arrangement may have been sanctioned by Alfred's father or by the Witan itself who guarded against the danger of a dispute regarding the succession should Æthelred fall in battle. This was a tradition among many Germanic peoples, such as the Swedes and Franks to whom we Anglo-Saxons are closely related. We Saxons crowned our successors from within the ranks of royal princes or, as the Romans did, choose from the best military commanders. This approach does seem logical to me, but in Alfred's case he was both a prince and a gifted warrior.'

Æthelstan fell silent. Without a word of warning he suddenly turned to look at me. Wearing a sullen expression, he deliberately changed the subject.

'Remember young Alder. Not a word about those damn silly cakes, for it upsets my grandmother.'

I, like most of the palace, had heard the rumours. It was common knowledge, but the whispers were only repeated inside the various stone corridors and hallways of Maeldunesburh Hall, and then only when the king was out of earshot.

I didn't know how to react to his mentioning of the gossip, and I tried to keep a straight face. I feared that any wrath might fall upon me, but I need not have worried, as Æthelstan burst into hysterical laughter.

'Grandfather told me that a king has more to worry about than burning cakes! However, rest assured there is no truth in the rumour. It is pure kitchen gossip.'

With that he beckoned me to follow him into his private chambers. 'Time to start our work, young Alder.'

I followed Æthelstan into an anti-chamber I had never seen before. The room was cold and bare, apart from a square table and two stools. Books and scrolls surrounded every wall from floor to ceiling. It was clear that Æthelstan was comfortable in these surroundings, this room alone set in a vast labyrinth of chambers and passageways. In this one small austere space the King could rest and unwind interrupted. Æthelstan waved his arms about, beckoning me to view what was on display.

'This is our history,' he said. 'If these books and scrolls should fall into the hands of the Pagan Vikings, then what we had learnt from the Celtic-Britons and Roman ancestors, and possibly our Saxon beliefs, will be burnt to ashes. The north men have no use for history! All they live for is to kill and enslave their enemies and to forcibly bind us to their pagan gods. My grandfather nearly lost Wessex, and all of the other kingdoms had been forced to submit to the yoke of the Norsemen from Scandinavia.'

Æthelstan's appeared lost in thought, as if he was thinking about years gone by. An anguished look spread over his face as he recalled his grandfather's struggle to retake his kingdom, the last kingdom.

Alfred was born in 849 at The Royal Palace in Wantage, Oxanforda, as the youngest son of King Æthelwulf, or as he liked to be called, the Noble Wolf of Wessex. It seemed improbable he would ever become king. The Vikings were not a threat to Wessex during Æthelwulf's reign, but in 843, he was defeated in a battle against the Vikings at Carhampton in Sumorsaete. Within a decade Æthelwulf achieved a major victory at the Battle of Aclea. He appointed his eldest surviving son Æthelbald to act as King of Wessex in his absence, and his other son Æthelberht to rule Cantaware, a shire in the south-eastern corner of Briton we call Cent or Cantia.

Æthelwulf and Æthelstan spent a year in Rome with the Mercian Æthelflæd, and upon his return he married Judith, the daughter of the West Frankish king. When Æthelwulf returned to Wessex, Æthelbald refused to surrender the West Saxon throne, and Æthelwulf for the sake of peace reluctantly agreed to divide his kingdom into two parts. He retained the east and left the west in

Æthelbald's hands. On Æthelwulf's death in 858 Wessex was left to Æthelbald and Cent to Æthelberht, but when Æthelbald died two years later. Æthelberht moved to reunify the kingdom of Wessex.

Æthelstan paused to make sure I was keeping up with his dialogue. 'Are you writing down all that I speak? I apologise for the similarity in our ancestors' names, but that was our tradition.'

I simply nodded to inform the king that everything he had said had been faithfully recorded but I did not admit that sometimes it was hard to keep up.

'Then let me continue, young Alder.'

'At the beginning of this century, Wessex and our neighbours were almost completely under Saxon rule, with Mercia and ourselves being the most dominant and powerful of the southern kingdoms. Mercia was dominant until the 820's, and it exercised overlordship over East Anglia and Cent, but Wessex was able to maintain its independence from Mercia.

'Sadly, almost nothing of importance was recorded during the first twenty years of Æthelberht's reign, apart from his campaigns against Cornwalum. There were minor skirmishes but nothing of real importance was written in the seven kingdoms during those two decades, except when the Isles of Sheppey in Cent were ravaged. In fact, in those days Sheppey was made up of two self-ruling separate regions, the Isle of Harty to the south east and the Isle of Elmley to the south west. The Viking raiders took full advantage of Sheppey. They slaughtered the local breeding herd of cattle and wintered on the island, stealing food and raping the women. They outstayed there welcome.

You will now understand why it is so important for me to have a true record of our past. We need to know more about our ancestors, our achievements and our failures, and to learn from our mistakes. I freely admit there have been a few catastrophes, otherwise this account would be deceitful but, apart from the Danes, our lives have been reasonably peaceful and good.'

Æthelstan rested his elbows on the table and supported his face with both hands, looking weary. As I looked across the table towards him, I could see he looked troubled, but felt it wasn't my place to say anything. It was up to the King to tell me when he had finished for the day. I peered out of the solitary window to view the scene outside. Snow was falling and settling everywhere. Æthelstan noticed what I was doing and made a comment.

'This is the best time of the year, young Alder, for it is a time of peace and prayer. No Viking of note would ever consider attacking us in the winter months and, what's more, it is a time of religious meditation and celebration of Jesus Christ, our Saviour.'

Æthelstan stood up, and I knew it was my duty to stand with him. If a king stood everybody stood, but Æthelstan bade me to sit down again.

'You can check your manuscript for any errors before you sleep. I must be off for evening prayers.'

With that he slowly walked from the room, leaving me to assemble the pages and to make sure they were all in correct order.

Saxon warrior

Chapter 2

The Wanderer

'The Wanderer'

Translated from Anglo-Saxon by Jeffrey Hopkins

Often the lonely receives love
the Creator's help, though heavy with care
over the sea he suffers long
stirring his hands in the frosty swell, the way of exile.
Fate never wavers.
The wanderer spoke. He told his sorrows,
the deadly onslaughts, the death of the clan,
at dawn alone I must mouth my cares.

The man does not live whom I dare tell my depths straight
out
I see truth in the lordly custom
for the courageous man to bind fast his breast.

Loyal to his treasure closet, thoughts aside
the weary cannot control fate or do bitter thoughts settle
things.
The eager for glory often bind something bloody close to
their breasts.

Spring came early in the year 930. Æthelstan was keen to continue his great work, but this had to be put on hold due to his duties overseeing the farmsteads. This obligation carried with it the taking of an accurate census of every animal - cattle and sheep, especially the new-born lambs.

We had an excellent lambing season. We Saxons base our farming year on the lunar calendar. The months are marked by the phases of the moon hence we derive the name monath from the word Mona, meaning the moon. As a result, the year is made of 354 days. This obviously results in an accumulation of days at the end of every couple of years for which a thirteenth month is added to our year. When this occurs the first full moon in the extra month is called a blue moon, the year being referred to as '*þæs monan gear*' or the moon year.

Æthelstan was always disappointed when unforeseen delays to his chronicle slowed it to a complete stand-still, but he knew everybody had to attend to their duties in the fields, even the king. Then one morning I was summoned.

'Alder, if you are ready to continue our great work, I have free time this afternoon. I have memories of Alfred and Æthelred's heroism I wish you to commit to parchment.' Æthelstan behaved like a mischievous young boy at these times. His love of accuracy was paramount and, as far as he was concerned, the sooner it was put down on parchment the better.

'Write this down exactly as I dictate, for I wish to tell you more about the Great Heathen Army.

'Grandfather was recorded as fighting alongside his brother Æthelred in a failed attempt to keep the Great Heathen Army, led by Ivar the Boneless, out of the adjoining Kingdom of Mercia. However, at the end of nine engagements, all fighting stopped as winter set in, ending with mixed results.

The places and dates of two of these battles were never recorded, hence my reasoning for this chronicle. As there seems to be no account of these battles, I assume we lost them both; otherwise our chroniclers would have recorded them in glorious song, colour, poems and words.

We did enjoy a successful skirmish at the Battle of Englefield in Berrocshire around the final days of Aerra Geola in the year 870, which was unfortunately followed soon afterwards by a devastating defeat at Readingum at the hands of Ivan's brother Haldane Ragnarsson on the fifth day of Aeftera Geola 871. We Saxons fought back and shattered the Danes with a devastating victory at the Battle of Ashdown on the Berrocshire Downs, at Compton near Aldworth. Grandfather was particularly accredited with the success of this last battle, but we

Saxons were forced to swallow our pride after another shock defeat at the Battle of Basing later that same month. We suffered another defeat during the month of Hredmonath in that same year at Merton but, due to the scribe's dreadful spidery handwriting, we couldn't properly decipher his words. The battle might have been at Morden in Wiltunscir or Martin in Dorset.

In Eostremonath of the year 871, my great uncle, King Æthelred, died at Wimborne Minster, leaving Alfred free to accede to the throne of Wessex. This carried a heavy burden as we needed to repair its defences. Æthelred left two under-age sons, the ætheling Æthelwold and Æthelhelm. The brothers had previously agreed at a Witenaġemot held at Swinbeorg that the sibling who outlived the other would inherit the personal property that King Æthelwulf had left jointly to his sons in his will. The sons would receive only whatever property and riches their father had settled upon them and whatever additional lands their uncle had acquired. The brothers also agreed that the surviving brother would be crowned king. Because of the recent Viking invasions and the tender age of his nephews, grandfather's accession probably went uncontested.

It was not a good time to accede to the throne, for it was a time of death and destruction. It looked as though the Saxon race would forever be enslaved or even wiped from the face of this land. We were the last kingdom within Saxon Briton, and our kingdom was getting smaller by the day. Unless a miracle was forthcoming the dream of a kingdom of Englaland would be forever lost. We would live in constant fear, if living that be, and we Saxons would live under the yoke of the Danelaw. However, every Saxon of noble birth knew they would either be exiled or put to the sword. These were truly our darkest years.

Between Easter and Whitsuntide, Grandfather emerged from the marsh lands of Sumorsaete and rode to the symbolic stone of Egbert, east of Selwood where he was met by his loyal supporters from Sumorsaete and Wiltunscir. Some had joined the Saxon forces from as far away as Hamtunscir which is near the channel waters, west of Hamptunr.

A great cheer went up as his supporters viewed Alfred's re-emergence from his marshland stronghold. It all seemed to be a carefully planned offensive that entailed raising the fyrds of three shires, which meant that not only had the king retained the loyalty of ealdormen, royal reeves and thegns, who were charged with levying and leading his warriors, but that they had maintained their positions of authority within their respective locations well enough to answer Alfred's summons for war.

Æthelstan confirmed Alfred's actions of retaining good intelligence with the use of scouts and secret messengers.

Preparation and bravery were more important than the actual deed, and they won the day when King Alfred overwhelmed the Danes in the ensuing Battle at Ethandun near Westbury, Wiltunscir. Alfred and his earls had devised a tactic to overwhelm the Danes, one that he studied from reading about the old Roman campaigns. Instead of the usual shield wall formation which relied on men holding fast and trusting his nearest companion to hold fast, Alfred considered the use of a totally new formation known as the arrowhead. At two hundred yards both armies adopted the shield wall, but Alfred had trained his men to move fast and to change from one formation into another within a short period of time, for speed was of the essence.

At Ethandun, on a grassy damp slope, Guthrum lined up his warriors in the tried and tested shield wall. At the commencement of the battle Alfred adopted a similar pose, but when the gap between the two forces shortened to less than one hundred yards Alfred, who was stationed within the centre of his men, ordered his shield wall to alter formation into the arrowhead. The Romans had varying degrees of success with this tactic. The Vikings had never witnessed this tactic before and panicked as bewilderment sunk into their drunken heads.

Most of their front line ceased moving forward, unsure what to do next. Chaos ensued as the second and third ranks got entangled with their own front line. Alfred and his disciplined warriors pushed forward gathering pace, whilst the Danes wavered. The old shield wall strategy had normally given the Danes a quick victory. It was basically a push and thrust, stab and hack, spit, swear and abuse your enemy approach. The louder they cursed at their opponent the more confidence grew, but their secret was to eat the fly agaric mushrooms and drink to excess prior to any battle. The force of the arrowhead propelling itself forward onto an uncertain line brought panic to the Danes. They attempted to outflank the cheering Saxons, but as they tried our arrowhead rotated meaning that fresh men would always pierce their ever-wavering front line. Within minutes the Viking lines had lost their momentum. They were no longer swearing and cursing at us Saxons, but at themselves. Unable to fully distinguish friend from foe, their line broke and the arrow pushed a wide gap into their force. Guthrum and his standard bearers were isolated and pushed further and further away from their fellow countrymen.

As soon as Alfred witnessed the confusion amongst the Viking ranks, he released his mounted spearmen to begin their horrific work of stabbing the unprotected bodies of the enemy. With the dead and wounded scattered about the battlefield, Saxon and Dane alike, the horsemen began to enjoy their work, thinking it better to kill the invader than show mercy. The bright green grass was churned up by the mud from the horse's hooves and quickly turned red with blood. Detached limbs, headless corpses were all mixed with guts and intestines, and numerous other body parts began to pile high within the centre of the field. The final insult for the Danes was the need to flee, but there was nowhere to run. Alfred had turned Ethandun into a field of horror, a field of dead men. Some survivors felt reassured that, at least for a few precious seconds, they were still alive, but a spear could still slam into any backbone, leaving moral fibre trampled on the field of death.

Alfred pursued the Danes to their stronghold at Chippenham and starved them into submission. One of the terms of Guthrum's surrender was his conversion to Christianity. It seemed unlikely at the time but three weeks later the Danish king and most of his chief men were baptised at Alfred's court at Aller, near Athelney. With the signing of the Treaty between Alfred and Guthrum two years later, Guthrum's people began settling in East Anglia, to becoming peaceful farmers. Alfred had forever neutralised Guthrum as a threat. A second Viking force, which had wintered at Fulanhamme, made a hasty retreat and sailed to Ghent where they settled to become a thorn in the side of the Flemish speaking people.

I stopped writing as I noticed a tear fall gently down Æthelstan cheek. I had never seen the king in such an emotional state before.

Æthelstan looked drained. He was lost in Alfred's memories, and it was clear those memories had cut him deeper than any sword. Æthelstan cleared his throat as if he wanted to continue his narrative, but instead he stood. Without a word, he vanished from his private chamber.

I was completely alone, too afraid to stand or touch any of his precious possessions. I glanced over my notes making minor adjustments to his narrative whilst trying to understand the king's dubious state of mind. It seemed that he was attempting to recall, but at the same time trying to forget the horrors that would forever haunt him. Although he had not witnessed Ethandun or Chippenham himself, he was constantly troubled by thoughts of an enemy whose sole intention was to eliminate his family and everything they stood for. The Viking forces on that day very nearly attained their goal, and all I could do was wait until he regained his composure to describe the torments that had been his living nightmares all those years.

Æthelstan had not been born when the royal court presided over a disease-ridden, inhospitable boggy marshland near Athelney in Sumorsaete. The Viking army under King Guthrum withdrew to Readingum and the old Roman city of Lundene. I knew this from the former chroniclers, but I needed Æthelstan to confirm or deny the rumours that Alfred paid a bounty to the Danes to persuade them to leave Wessex, but he never confirmed or denied this.

Guthrum must have considered himself unbeatable. He had a large army at his disposal ready to slaughter the remnants of Alfred's Saxon force, as well as our wagons filled to overflowing with Saxon treasure. It wouldn't have been too much of a problem to finish us off whenever he wanted, but Guthrum bided his time. Perhaps he was overconfident and waited too long, and that surely was his biggest mistake.

Our chronicle had to be delayed until Æthelstan was ready to continue with it. I automatically said 'our' chronicle.

I know it is Æthelstan's chronicle, put down on parchment by me, Alder, but as I have been so involved with the work it seems right to speak of this great work as 'ours'. Of course, I would never speak about the chronicle in this way in front of my king.

The Saxon battle-axe

The shield wall formation used by the Danes proved
ineffectual against the Saxons
flying wedge at Ethandun.

The arrowhead formation known as the Boar's Snout, or
Swine's Array, or flying wedge could easily break through
the shield wall.

Chapter 3

A Troubled Æthelstan

Often the lone-dweller awaits his own favour,
the Measurer's mercy, though he must,
mind-caring, throughout the ocean's way
stir the rime-chilled sea with his hands
for a long while, tread the tracks of exile.
The way of the world is ever an open book.

So spoke the earth-stepper, mindful of miseries,
slaughter of the wrathful, crumbling of kinsmen.

Often alone, every daybreak, I must bewail my cares.
There is now no one living to whom I dare articulate my
mind's grasp.
I know as truth that it is a noble custom
for a man to enchain his spirit's close,
to hold his hoarded coffer, think what he will.

Nor can the weary mind withstand these outcomes,
nor can a troubled heart effect itself help.
Therefore those eager for glory will often
secure a sorrowing mind in their breast-coffer,
just as I must fasten in fetters my heart's ken,
often wretched, deprived of my homeland,
far from freeborn kindred, since years ago.

When Æthelstan felt relaxed and comfortable enough to continue his great work, he showed renewed excitement about the chronicle. He hoped it would bring light and understanding to Saxon Briton, a country we constantly dreamed of calling Englaland.

'When I was only four or five years old my grandfather died. His death brought a fear to Wessex and Mercia, and to my father, King Edward, Alfred's successor. King Edward thought the Norsemen would choose war over peace and again offer challenges to the Saxons in their supremacy over the southern shires of Briton, but there remained an uneasy state of calm until Æthelwold made an outlandish claim to the throne. Edward had expected a declaration of war to come from the Danes, but he hadn't contemplated a revolt from his own cousin. Æthelwold ætheling tried to seize the Saxon throne from my father. It finally ended when Æthelwold was killed in battle at Holme while fighting alongside his stinking Viking allies. You can always bet on your own family to create mayhem at home.

Æthelwold's initial move was to take a small force and seize Wimborne, in Dormdaete, Æthelred's final resting place. Æthelwold took control of the crown lands at Dormdaete before returning to Wimborne to await Edward's response. Edward assembled his army and marched them along the old Roman road to the fort town of Bradbury.

Æthelwold refused to meet my father in open battle. Instead he stayed with his men at Wimborne where he kidnapped a nun, seemingly preparing for a long stand-off.

Although Æthelwold had the resources for a full-frontal assault, and even prepared his army to attack, he unexpectedly abandoned his warriors and rode north during the night. Edward assumed his cousin rode north to reinforce his men with Viking's from Northanhymbre. Æthelwold appealed for support from the Danish kingdom of Northanhymbre and unsurprisingly they pledged their allegiance to the upstart. Coins were minted during this period proclaiming Æthelwold as the puppet king of Jórvík. Meanwhile, Edward was crowned king at the King's Stone by the Temes.

Edward was afterwards heard to have commented about Æthelwold, 'better be a living coward than a dead hero'. When the battle eventually took place Æthelstan was too young to remember Edward's words which may have been fabricated, and in any case Æthelstan was not present at the battle. Civil war seemed inevitable.

In the autumn of 901, Æthelwold sailed his fleet, aided by his new allies into Bemfleot, East Seaxna. In the early months of the following year he and his East Anglian Danes attacked deeper into Mercia, one assault being the twenty-fifth burh of Cricklade, in Wiltunscir.

Edward retaliated by ravaging East Anglia. When he retreated, the men of Cent disobeyed his orders to retire, and gave battle against the Danes in the nearby shire of Huntandun, at the Battle of the Holme in the month of Aerrala that same year.

Although Æthelwold and his Danish East Anglian allies defeated Edward's troops, as a result of the battle both Æthelwold and Eohric, the Danish king of East Anglia, were killed in the ensuing slaughter. There were considerable losses on the Saxon side, including his two Centish ealdormen, Sigehelm and Sigewulf.

Many thought my father, King Edward, had made a major error in failing to fully engage the Danes with his whole army at Holme, leading to recriminations that threatened his authority, particularly in Cent. No blame could be placed upon my shoulders, for I was only a young boy at the time and barely able to hold a sword.

During the following year in excess of two hundred Viking ships landed in the Lympne Estuary in Cent and a smaller force successfully landed further up the Temes estuary, under the command of the Danish King Hastein. These were reinforced by ships from the settled Danes of East Anglia and some of their contingent sailed further around our southern coast to besiege two burh towns, both in Dyfneint.

Edward reorganised his burh's and defences inside Wessex and organised the conception of a navy, as well as a standing army. Like his father, he built a series of fortified burhs that ringed our boundaries and these burhs sprang up throughout our kingdom. To maintain the burhs, and the Saxon standing army, Edward set up a taxation system he called the Burghal Hidage.

Viking raids continued but our newly reinforced defences proved too much for the Vikings, so they made no further impact. I remember my father boasting about his exploits at the Battle of Buttington in Powys when an army of Saxons, together with their Welsh allies, defeated the Danes under the command of Hastein.

The Saxon thegns assembled an immense combined army of Saxons and Welsh. The collective army under King Edward's command laid siege to the Vikings who had hastily built a fortification at Buttington. After several weeks the starving Vikings broke out of their fortification, only to be beaten by the combined English and Welsh army with many of the Vikings being put to the sword and axe. We lived in a continuous state of war but eventually a prolonged period of peace shone over the land. It felt good to wake up in the morning without worrying about packing weapons, but my father knew the Danes would never remain peaceable for long.

So, just after my fifteenth birthday in the year 910, I rode with my father to 'Wulfruna's town on the great hill,' better known to the Dane and Saxon alike as Wōdnesfeld. Our exact target was the small sheltered town of Tettenhall where our scouts informed us that the Danes had set up their camp. The Danes had called the town after one of their ancestors named Teotta.

The Danelaw kings assembled their fleet and transported their army, via the River Saefern, directly into the heartland of Mercia. There they ravaged the land and plundered large amounts of valuable booty. They quickly sought a return to their native north before the combined armies of Mercia and West Saxons caught them strung out on the march from Wōdnesfeld.

We did not know it at the time but the Battle of Tettenhall was a turning point against the Danish invaders. The united forces of my father, Edward of Wessex, and Ealdorman Æthelred of Mercia, witnessed the crushing defeat against the last of the large Viking armies to ravage Saxon lands, but that was before I knew of Brunanburh. It was at Tettenhall where I had my first kill, although you could hardly call it a kill, as the unsuspecting Dane accidently ran onto my spear.

Unable to retreat, the Viking kings leading the raid - Ingwær, Eowils and Healfdan - were all killed by our warriors. We Saxon's shed not one tear over their loss, for there would be other battles to win, and other Viking warriors to kill. My father told me afterwards that many thousands of Danes died on that day. Our casualty figures, although high, were far lower than theirs. Tettenhall stirred memories within my own heart, for it was there that my brothers died whilst carrying the Wessex banners.

As Æthelstan continued his narrative I stopped writing. It was the first time I had ever heard him glorifying death. I knew the Danes didn't expect to be given or offered quarter, but I had not expected Æthelstan to specify the gruesome ways the Vikings met their deaths. I raised my hand to question Æthelstan regarding where the Danes said they travelled to in their afterlife.

'Sire, is there any truth in the rumour that, according to Viking legend, only the bravest men killed in battle but still holding their swords would enter their Valhalla? Do they hope to stand alongside Odin and, when time is no more, fight each other in one final glorious battle with the Gods?'

Æthelstan smiled. 'I too have heard that silly gossip, but remember this, young Alder. The Viking legend also states that at the point when the sand in the hour glass has expelled, known to them as the age of Ragnarok, every unholy giant and demon known to man will finally breach the walls of Asgard and wage war on those left living. Therefore, there seems little point in travelling to a Pagan heaven to fight with your Gods as, if you are successful, you will afterwards fight your worst kind of nightmare in the form of demons and giants ascending from hell!'

I smiled back. It did seem rather ridiculous now that Æthelstan had answered my question, but he followed it with a further comment. 'No more questions, young Alder, especially about their God Thor conjuring up thunder with his war hammer. It is just a way of keeping young boys like you under control.'

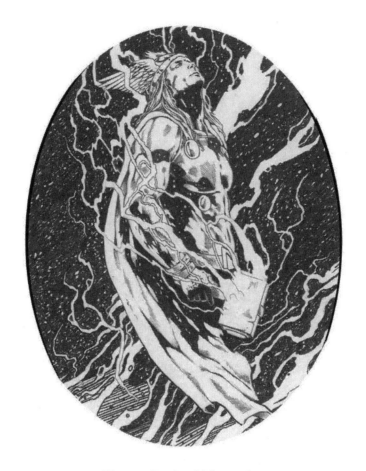

Thor, God of Thunder

Thor's hammer

Chapter 4

Murky Clouds Above

I gathered my gold-friend in earthen gloom,
and went forth from there abjected,
winter-anxious over the binding of waves,
hall-wretched, seeking a dispenser of treasure,
where I, far or near, could find him who
in the mead-hall might know of my kind,
or who wishes to comfort a friendless me,
accustomed as he is to joys.

The experienced one knows how cruel
sorrow is as companion,
he who has few adored protectors
the paths of the exile claim him,
not wound gold at all a frozen spirit-lock,
not at all the fruits of the earth.
He remembers hall-retainers and treasure-taking,
how his gold-friend accustomed him
in his youth to feasting. Joy is all departed!
Therefore he knows who must long forgot

the counsels of beloved lord,
when sleep and sorrow both together
constrain the miserable loner so often.
It seems to him in his mind that he embraces
and kisses his lord, and lays both hands and head
on his knee, just as he sometimes
in the days of yore delighted in the gift-throne.
Then he soon wakes up, a friendless man,
seeing before him the fallow waves,
the sea-birds bathing, fanning their feathers,
ice and snow falling down, mixed with hail.

Soon after sunrise the following morning a line of dark clouds ominously appeared on the distant horizon. Devilish murky clouds seemed to rise through the freshly ploughed earth to offer a bizarre frown, telling me that Thor, the Viking God of thunder, wasn't fooling around. Everything then went calm and a deathly silence roared inside my head, my brain aching with pounding pain. It wasn't only me who had heard the silence. The birds on the wing who had previously been merrily chirping away since before dawn abruptly hushed themselves and flew to the safety of their nesting grounds. At the same time our chickens scattered in panic, but there was no safety for them even as they huddled together for protection.

I found it intriguing that we Britons have recognized for centuries what we call the calm before the expected storm. The Danes apparently thought that someone had displeased the Gods to such an extent that Thor himself would whip up the wind and plunge the air temperatures. Then he would make his glorious entrance to rumbles of thunder, before the storm took hold to create a tumultuous downpour. Those still sleeping in their beds of straw might drown if they remained unprepared for the wrath of Thor, but that morning it all seemed very different.

The misty sunrise took on an eerie silence which seemed to last forever. Although we all knew what to expect, every living soul jumped with fear when the crack of thunder finally came to shake the ground and uproot some of the trees. The rain came in torrents, plummeting as though the water from every nearby river, lake and stream on Saxon land was being thrown down upon our heads by the living ghost of Thor - or could it be our own patriarch Noah?

Bishop Aldhelm had often spoken of Noah who was a righteous man and walked with God. Seeing that our earth was corrupt and filled with violence, God instructed Noah to build a large boat in which he, his sons, and their wives, together with a male and female of all the living creatures known on earth, would be saved from the deluge. Noah laboured for over five decades to build his Ark and many people poked fun at him, thinking him crazy.

It rained for forty days and nights, concealing every mountain and landmark known to man on earth. When the rains ceased, Noah set a raven free to see if the flood waters had subsided, and if there was anything on which the raven could land, but the raven failed to return. A few days later Noah released a dove, and lo and behold the dove returned to Noah with a small olive branch in his beak. Noah knew that somewhere dry land existed, and that the waters were slowly abating.

Bishop Aldhelm explained that the story of Noah in the Bible told us that much of the earth's troubles were caused by wicked angels who left heaven to have relations with women on earth. These angels had offspring called Nephilim, who wreaked havoc on humankind. In the book of Genesis, God decided to clear the earth of wickedness and to only allow good people to have a fresh start in life. Of the many stories Bishop Aldhelm told I particularly liked the story of Noah, mainly because the Bishop often told me that I was a good person. What is more, to the best of my knowledge, Bishop Aldhelm never built any kind of Ark during his lifetime, but if he ever considered such a mammoth task, I would be the first to stand beside my friend to offer my services. The people thought Aldhelm's stories were just that - stories, legends and myths - but I wasn't sure. I had always been told that God never lied, so the story of Noah must be true.

Bishop Aldhelm once told me the Gospel writers, Matthew and Luke, recorded that Jesus mentioned Noah and the flood. The prophet Ezekiel and the apostle Paul cited Noah as an example of faith and righteousness. Aldhelm pointed out that it surely wouldn't make sense for any of these writers to choose a mythical person as an example to follow, but I digress.

When Thor's deluge finally came, it fell heavily for six days, leaving the ground a mud bath and curtailing any worthwhile warrior movements for either Dane or Saxon. This extreme downpour coincided with a great event close to the Roman Wall near the city of Ceaster.

Edward, Æthelstan and Aldhelm were all surprised with the news, but at the same time they were pleased as it brought Æthelflæd, the Lady of Mercia, into the affray. As he spoke, Æthelstan stressed the word Lady, for she was not a Queen, but was Alfred's daughter.

He explained he would talk at length on Ceaster later, but we had to wait until the land had dried sufficiently to allow our animals and wagons to move freely. We had to transport our winter feed to the Upper Green where the land was considerably higher and drier than within the confines of the village.

Æthelstan summoned his brothers, Edmund, Ælfweard, Edwin and Eadred, to join him the following day at Maeldunesburh Abbey for a hurriedly arranged gathering with his military advisors. Æthelflæd was invited but had to decline, due to a pressing engagement with the Danes.

Æthelflæd was the eldest daughter of King Alfred of Wessex. She was known to have been a strong, independent and well-educated princess. During her early years, Æthelflæd witnessed her father take back large swathes of Englaland from the Danes, starting with the famous battle of Ethandun in Wiltunscir, a key turning point in the Saxon campaign against the Vikings. Æthelflæd had been widowed when her husband Æthelred, Jarl of Mercia, died six years earlier.

Æthelred constantly turned to his West Saxon neighbour in the south. King Alfred of Wessex readily assisted him in the defence of his kingdom. Alfred agreed to help his kinsman, and in 886 he managed to secure the partially abandoned Roman city of Lundene back from the Danes.

Lundene had once been a Roman fortress at the south-eastern tip of Mercian territory. It had traditionally been a Mercian city but had constantly been sacked at the hands of the murderous Vikings. Alfred, as a token of his victory, handed the city back to Æthelred who, as a sign of his gratitude, agreed to sign an alliance with Alfred, a pact that effectively forced Mercia to acknowledge Wessex as the dominant Saxon power within central and southern Saxon territory. The deal was sealed when Alfred decided to marry off his eldest daughter Æthelflæd to the Mercian Æthelred, even though she was only around 16 years old at the time.

Within a few years, Æthelred and Æthelflæd had their first and only child, a daughter whom they called Ælfwynn. The years that followed witnessed the husband and wife team take back much Mercian land from the Danes, both in the Middle lands and in the north. Æthelstan confirmed that Æthelflæd brought a great deal of military might and strategy to the table, including the tactic of fortifying Mercian borders after they drove the Danes further north. Æthelstan held Æthelflæd in high esteem, and once told me that if he ever took a wife, someone in the mould of Æthelflæd would be perfection personified. She was beautiful, with long blonde hair flowing down to the nape of her back, but she had another important attribute – intelligence.

In the early years of her reign, Æthelflæd gave battle against a large band of Vikings outside the city of Ceaster. This group were refugees driven back from Ireland by an uprising in Dyflin. The Danes had sought permission to live peacefully and obey the Saxon laws, so they set up camp accordingly outside Ceaster, under the proviso that they behaved themselves. Unfortunately, the Vikings got restless, as we knew they would, and launched a couple of unsuccessful raids on the nearby city of Ceaster. Upon hearing of the Danes uprising in the area, Æthelflæd rode north to meet the Danes with a cunning battle plan. She would first fight the Vikings outside the city but would then fall back to draw the Vikings inside the city walls. Once inside, the gates would be shut tight. Those Danes caught within the confines of the city walls were slaughtered without mercy by Æthelflæd's warriors who had hid themselves inside the city.

Æthelred had not been involved in many of Æthelflæd's campaigns, as he had suffered from a severe sickness since the turn of the century. After ten years of war, combined with ill health, Æthelred finally died in 911. At this time Æthelflæd became the sole ruler of Mercia and was titled 'Lady of Mercia'. She was never given the title 'Queen of Mercia' because the Mercians hated the idea of any female becoming their ruler, although everyone thought she would have been an eminent leader.

During the following year, Æthelflæd continued to force the Danes out of the central and southern Saxon regions of what was to eventually become Englaland. Æthelflæd engaged them in Wales five years later, before moving north to Deor and Ledecestre. She crossed the River Humbre, and even managed to persuade the City of Eoferwic to pledge their allegiance to her. Æthelstan continued:

'My cousin was succeeded by her daughter Ælfwynn, but her reign was cut short on the orders of my brother, Edward, who ousted Ælfwynn and dissolved Mercia into the Kingdom of Wessex. Worried about any future Mercian uprisings, due to Ælfwynn's exile, my brother quickly quelled all Mercian resistance by forcing Ælfwynn to live the remainder of her life in a nunnery!

Æthelflæd died at Tamworth just two weeks before she had planned to visit Eoferwic and was later buried in St Oswald's Priory in Gloucester. Æthelflæd was dear to me, young Alder.' I squirmed at his description of me as 'young Alder' but what he said next softened my heart.

'If you could brighten her soul with gentle flowing words, I will forever be grateful to you.'

Æthelstan touched my shoulder gently and suggested it was time to eat and rest. 'There is another day tomorrow, when I will tell you about multiple Saxon raids led by Æthelflæd. These were carried out to forcibly remove the Danes from the middle-Saxon-lands and the north of our country, especially at Derbentio. You may know of it as the valley of the deer, but today, young Alder, we call it Dore. I will tell you much and you will faithfully write down my words and transfer them onto parchment.'

Alder

Chapter 5

In The Month of Aefteraliva

Then the hurt of the heart will be heavier,
painful after the beloved. Sorrow will be renewed.
Whenever the memory of kin pervades his mind,
he greets them joyfully,

Eagerly looking them up and down,
the companions of men they always swim away.
The spirits of seabirds do not bring many
familiar voices there. Cares will be renewed
for him who must very frequently send
his weary soul over the binding of the waves.

Therefore, a man cannot become wise,
before he has earned his share of
winters in this world.
A wise man ought to be patient,
nor too hot-hearted, nor too hasty of speech,
nor too weak a warrior, nor too foolhardy,
nor too fearful nor too fey, nor too coin-grasping,
nor ever too bold for boasting,
before he knows readily.

Æthelstan was up very early the following morning, and it was my duty to attend to his needs prior to my duties as scribe. He looked at me and smiled. 'I trust you had a good night's sleep, Alder, for I have much to tell about my cousin, the Lady of Mercia.

'In the month of Aefteraliva in the year 917, Æthelflæd launched a series of offensive forays into Deoraby, her target being the old Roman fortress. It was confirmed by our scouts that the Saxon ruler of Deoraby had aligned himself with the Norsemen. Sadly, there were plenty of fat Saxons who willingly sold themselves to the Danes in exchange for land, false titles and gold. To make matters worse, the Saxons and Vikings joined forces to create Deoraby, or whatever they call the stinking place, into one of the Five Boroughs within the Danelaw.'

I looked into Æthelstan's eyes and saw nothing but sadness. Confused, I asked a question. 'How could the Saxons and the venomous Danes work together in perfect harmony? I don't understand, for surely they should be lifelong enemies.'

'Let me continue without your interruptions, young Alder.'

There it was again! Did Æthelstan purposely rile me, or was he teasing me? Either way, I was certain he was enjoying himself at my expense. Æthelstan restarted his narrative.

Æthelflæd quickly saw that the defenders at Deoraby had grown lazy as well as fat. They had ignored the fact that their burh had not been reinforced, and parts of the defensive wall had been reduced to rubble. Æthelflæd simply walked through the debris and successfully assaulted the town within days. The Danes might have established their military headquarters at Deoraby. Their six-acre rectangular fort would have given the burh the equivalent of about 500 hides. The Vikings had camped at nearby Hrepandum in 874, although they had quickly abandoned it, but the Lady of Mercia had rapidly brought the town and surrounding countryside back under Mercian rule. The Danes either fled or pledged themselves to Æthelflæd's authority and the traitorous Saxons were quickly singled out and put to death for collaborating with the Danes. Whilst the honest, hard-working Saxons were pleased to be back under honest Mercian protection, I must confess I hate the idea of killing for the sake of killing, but one must be ruthless when dealing with traitors. Otherwise oaths given freely to a lord will be worthless, so they had to be taught a severe lesson.'

I looked up from the parchment to see a broad smile on Æthelstan's face. I couldn't help myself and laughed, for even in stories victories smell good. 'Victory is sweet, my Lord,' I said, and Æthelstan's grin confirmed my assessment.

'Have I mentioned the abbey and priory of Hrepandum?'' Æthelstan was clearly pleased with himself as his narrative came flooding back like the bore surge on the Saefern. *The great heathen army,*' he spat out the words as though they were vermin, 'wintered downstream of Hrepandum. The area is now simply a bog and almost permanently flooded but at the time of their filthy heathen army, and on holy ground, the local priest baptised Wystan of Mercia, later murdered by the Danes or his guardian. Such is the way of the Mercians. They have little honour compared to us men of Wessex.'

Æthelstan was clearly enjoying his continuous pranks aimed at Mercia. You must bear in mind that he was a Wessex man through and through. He was proud of Wessex and very much like his father, with Alfred's blood running hot through his veins.

'You are no doubt aware that after Æthelflæd sacked Hrepandum they discovered well over two hundred and fifty Viking graves buried in a pit beneath a large mound. None of them died in battle with their Viking swords in their hand, so Thor will be extremely pleased he has not got to fight these ghosts in his heathen paradise. The absence of battle scars suggests that they all died from a contagious disease. Well, all I can say is good riddance to bad rubbish.'

'I was not aware, my King, but it brings me much happiness to hear of their deaths.' I spoke truthfully and smiled, and Æthelstan seemed pleased to hear my words.

'You have to excuse me, Alder, for I was thinking about my ancestors who perished due to those murdering Vikings. I am more determined than ever to see our country known as Englaland or England, the land of the Angles. I would have no qualms or objections if the name be Briton or Britain, or Great Britain. The Romans once called our fair land Britannia. Now that does sound majestic and stately! Our lands will never be defeated again by any foreign invader. We Saxons will always see to that, and on this I pledge on my soul.'

I was concerned by Æthelstan's overconfidence, especially as his reign as King of Wessex had hardly begun, but I had to agree with him. It was the kind of speech that roused the ranks, the sort given before combat begins. Our leaders shouted passionately from a lofty position to inspire their supporters that God was on their side, yet I sometimes wondered if God knew whose side he was on. I could visualise Æthelstan, at sometime in the future, delivering such an exciting and stirring challenge to his warriors. If the challenge was greeted with enthusiasm his warriors would willingly die for his cause, but if the words failed to motivate, just keep a count of the number of deserters leaving the safety of the camp during the hours of darkness. If I were a judge of character, Æthelstan would always inspire his warriors. He was well respected by his fellow Saxons and I honestly think they would follow him through the gates of hell and beyond if asked.

In the year 918, in the village of Corbridge on the upper reaches of the River Tinan, two miles south of the Roman wall, the Norse-Gael leader Ragnall ua Ímair and his allies fought against the forces of Alba, in concert with Ealdred I of Bamburgh who had previously been driven out of Bernican lands by the much-despised Ragnall.

Æthelstan thought it strange that the Saxons allied themselves with the King of Alba, and stranger still that his Saxon scouts sent messages south to keep him informed. It seemed that Ragnall divided his forces into four separate columns, one of which was commanded by Jarl Ottir Iarla, a long-time ally of Ragnall. Ealdred of Bebbanburg had once been a close friend and ally of Æthelstan's father.

Reports on the battle were somewhat sketchy and difficult to comprehend, as the antagonists failed to grasp who they were fighting against. Our communication chain via a large stock of racing pigeons was hard pressed to convey accurate and speedy information.

Æthelstan remained south throughout the incursion, although he received frequent communications on how the battle progressed. Initially it appeared the

Scots had the upper hand as they destroyed the first three columns, but the fourth column remained intact.

Æthelstan wondered if this was a ploy to draw the Scots into an ambush, but he still didn't understand why Ragnall would sacrifice three columns of warriors to gamble on the outcome of the last column proving victorious, but victorious they were. The fourth and final column broke free and fell upon the Scottish-Saxon force in what can only be described as a perfect ambush melee.

The fortunes of the battle remained indecisive. Ragnall remained Master of Bamburgh, but for the northern part which had once been Bernicia and the southern regions of Deira. Perhaps both remained under Saxon influence; such was the problematic outcome of the battle of Coria.

'Make a note of Coria. One day I will make amends on behalf of the Saxon people who died that day. One day our lands will become united! Coria might be just another battle, but by God I will make Ragnall pay for his outrage, then that day will be mine.'

Æthelstan pushed out his chest and tightened his face muscles as he partially repeated those final words in anger: 'That day will be mine!'

The Scots managed to escape the field of battle without too much adversity. It seems that Æthelstan was right in predicting the result of the engagement at Coria as being indecisive. His problem was that it allowed Ragnall to re-establish himself further inside Saxon lands, and in the following year Ragnall descended on Eoferwic, which he took with great loss of life and had himself proclaimed king. The Bernicia's remained under his kingship, although Ealdred I of Bamburgh and Downfall I, king of Strath Clota, remained for a time faithful to Æthelstan, the king of Wessex.

Chapter 6

Yuletide is coming

A stout-hearted warrior ought to wait,
when he makes a boast, until he readily knows
where the thoughts of his heart will veer.

A wise man ought to perceive how ghostly it will be
when all this world's wealth stands wasted,
so now in various places throughout this middle-earth,
the walls stand, blown by the wind,
crushed by frost, the buildings snow-swept.

The winehalls molder, their wielder lies
deprived of joys, his peerage all perished,
proud by the wall. War destroyed some,
ferried along the forthway, some a bird bore away
over the high sea, another the grey wolf
separated in death, another a teary-cheeked
warrior hid in an earthen cave.

Yuletide is coming in just a few days' time,' Æthelstan reminded me, with more than a hint of jollity in his voice. 'Also, there are the celebrations to honour Saint Egwin of Evesham that preceded our winter solstice.' Not that I needed reminding of Yuletide.

In Saxon Briton we celebrate Saint Alburga's day or Saint Æthelberht's as we once knew her. Alburga's of Wilton was a Queen in Wessex until her death in the year of our Lord 810.

'In Saxon Briton we seem to honour more Saints than days of the year! The feast days of Egwin and Alburga are the best, for these are the times when our families get together to give and receive presents, eat, drink and generally enjoy ourselves.'

'What will you be eating on Saint Alburga's day?' Æthelstan enquired. I thought for a moment before answering, feeling slightly embarrassed. 'Vegetable stew, Sire, but what will you be having?'

'Probably wild boar or deer,' he replied with more than a hint of apathy.

'I worry about my brother's health, Alder. He seems constantly distant and remote from me and I find it difficult to talk with him. I fear the wars with the Danes weigh heavy on his mind. Edward conquered the Viking-ruled southern Briton in partnership with his sister and still we have the makings of another Mercian-Welsh revolt at Ceaster. It worries me that this could be one conflict too many for Edward.'

I could see Æthelstan's torment and suggested that he invite the three remaining brothers to spend the Yuletide together. 'We live in modern times, your Majesty. Giuli is a time for family gatherings, be you pauper or king.'

I was concerned that I might have spoken too freely. After all I am only a lowly scribe, and there are certain rules that apply when talking to a king. My worries disappeared, however, when I saw Æthelstan nodding in agreement with my suggestion.

'I will send messages to King Edward and my brothers Ælfweard, Edwin and Edmund. I will invite them and their families to join me here at Maeldunesburh for the Yuletide celebrations. I think next year will be an excellent year! You must come too, Alder,' he said excitedly.

'I fear I must decline, Sire. The thought of celebrating with you is most tempting but I must think of my widowed mother. I am her only family since my two brothers died at Tettenhall, so I am all she has left.'

'Then the invitation is extended to your mother.'

After putting down the revolt at Ceaster, Edward died from his wounds inflicted at Tettenhall in Ceaster on the seventeenth day of Aeferaliva 924 with Æthelstan by his side. Ælfweard our eldest half-brother died at Wessex sixteen days after the king. We deliberately kept the reason behind our king's death and that of my half-brother secret as we didn't wish to give the Vikings any comfort in knowing that they had slain both the King of Wessex and his heir. I, therefore, reluctantly accepted the throne. I was crowned King of Wessex, but that was not enough for me. I wanted our country to be united, so I needed to be crowned King of Britannia, Englaland or England. It didn't matter what the name was as long as we were all English.'

Æthelstan raised his eyes towards the heavens and with a faint smile on his lips and said, 'Glorious Englaland! Now that would be a most welcome present at this time of year. Don't you agree, young Alder?'

After his coronation, Æthelstan centralised his government. He increased the control over the production of charters and charges and summoned leading figures from distant areas to his councils. He invited rulers from outside his territory, especially the Cornwalum kings, who grudgingly acknowledged his overlordship and legal reforms which were founded on those proposed by his grandfather, Alfred. Due to its symbolic location on the border between the two kingdoms of Wessex and Mercia, his coronation took place on the fourth day of Haligmonath 925 on the King's stone at Kingston by the banks of the Temes River. Æthelstan was crowned by

Athelm, the Archbishop of Contwaraburg, but he really wanted to be crowned at Maeldunesburh. That was his adopted home and where he was happiest. One detail was changed by the Archbishop, who placed a crown of gold upon his head instead of his war helmet.

I must sadly state that opposition against his rule continued even after his coronation. The main antagonist was Frithestan, the Bishop of Wintancaester, who refused to attend his coronation or witness any of his charters for three long years. Thereafter he attended court regularly until Æthelstan accepted his resignation in 931.

'Why did the Bishop of Wintancaester refuse to attend your coronation, Sire?' I enquired.

'Perhaps he thought I murdered Ælfweard,' he replied.

'And did you, Sire?'

'Alder, I am a man of God and mercy. I would never think about murdering anyone.'

Æthelstan saw that I was troubled by this answer so tried to reassure me.

'I would never kill Ælfweard for he was very dear to me. Mind you, murdering Edmund or Edwin has crossed my mind.' In response I covered my mouth to stop myself from laughing and instinctively knew my king was telling the truth.

Æthelstan tried to reconcile the aristocracy to his Saxon rule. He lavished gifts on the minsters of Beverley, Chester-le-Street, and Eoferwic, principally to clearly stress his Christianity. In addition, Æthelstan purchased the vast Lancashire territory of Hacmunderness, bordered by Leyland to the south, Blackburn to the east and Lonsdale to the north. Afterwards he gave the land to Wolfstan, the Archbishop of Eoferwic, or as the Danes called it Jorvik. The Archbishop was his most trusted lieutenant in the northern regions, but Æthelstan remained a resented outsider.

The northern kingdoms preferred to ally themselves with the pagan Norsemen of Dyflin. In contrast to his strong control over southern Britain, his position north of the Humbre was far too fragile. Æthelstan could only resolve the dispute by taking it by force.

Æthelstan told me that his great chronicle had to be delayed whilst his mind was on other matters. I knew he meant the problems in the northern kingdoms as he spoke of little else. Once he even asked me what I would do in his position. Imagine that - a king asking for his scribe's advice!

As well as the northern kingdoms Æthelstan had other disputes to attend to, one being the Scottish kingdoms. Owen, King of Strath Clota, and King Constantine II of Alba had aligned themselves with the usurper king of Dyflin - Olaf Guthfrithson.

An alliance was forged between the three leaders so that, when they considered the time to be right, they would attack me as one and their wish to rid the land of Saxon dominance would be complete, but I will talk on that another day.

I had been Æthelstan's scribe for nearly twenty years, ten of which spent with him as my king. Our friendship grew to such an extent that we each knew the other's thoughts before speaking. I had been with him throughout the bad times, when his father and half-brothers had died, and stood with him when his armies had defeated the Viking invaders. His brother Edwin had drowned in the channel during a storm, and his body was washed ashore on the Francium coast. Yet again accusations grew that Æthelstan had played some part, but I knew differently, for I was there when Edwin and Æthelstan argued.

The reason I tell you this account is for the same reason Æthelstan instigated his chronicle, to keep a truthful record of Saxon history. I shall tell my version of events later within this chronicle. I knew other scribes had written of Edwin's death, one such being The Francium Annals Bertiniani, Compiled by Folcuin, it provides more detail:

'For in the year of the Incarnate Word 933, when the same King Edwin, driven by some disturbance in his kingdom, embarked on a ship, wishing to cross to this side of the sea, a storm arose and the ship was wrecked and he was overwhelmed in the midst of the waves. And when his body was washed ashore, Count Adelolf, since he was his kinsman, received it with honour and bore it to the monastery of Saint Bertin, at Saint-Omer for burial.'

I read the reported evidence with dismay, 'Sire,' I said. 'There is no independent account in this statement, which suggests it is nothing more than a fabricated lie. You are not blamed directly, but there is definitely a thinly-veiled accusation, suggesting your compliance in the tragedy.'

'I am fully aware of that fact, Alder,' he replied. 'But you know what they say – 'no smoke without fire.'

I was concerned for Æthelstan's health. His chronicle appeared to jump from one year to another before leaping further back in time, and I wondered if he was aware of his lack of coordination. I determined that I would sort this out during my rest periods and that his chronicle would appear to the reader as being nothing short of brilliant.

I worried about his last remark, however - 'no smoke without fire' – and pondered over it awhile.

Chapter 7

The Witenagemot

And so the Shaper of Men

Has laid this middle-earth to waste
until the ancient work of giants stood empty,
devoid of the revelry of their citizens.

Then he wisely contemplates this wall-stead
and deeply thinks through this darkened existence,
aged in spirit, often remembering from afar
many war-slaughterings, and he speaks these words

Where has the horse gone? Where is the man?
Where is the giver of treasure?
Where are the seats at the feast?
Where are the joys of the hall?
Alas the bright goblet! Alas the mailed warrior!
Alas the pride of princes!
How the space of years has passed
it grows dark beneath the night-helm,
as if it never was!

I had not seen Æthelstan for a few weeks and wondered if he was avoiding me, but after enquiring of his whereabouts I was told by his royal stewards that he was on a diplomatic mission visiting our neighbouring shires. I found this strange, but didn't think any more of it, until the early spring when riders started coming to Maeldunesburh.

First there were ten or twelve, and the banners and shield markings told me they were from the various Saxon held kingdoms. Finally Æthelstan himself rode back to the abbey which could only mean one thing. A Witenagemot or Witan or, in its simplest form, a gathering) had been called. I often wondered what went on inside such meetings but soon I would find out, for Æthelstan invited me to keep an accurate record of what was said, and who was truly on his side. It seemed to me that I was being asked to spy on the king's unsuspecting guests, including the Ealdormen.

Æthelstan had called the Witan on the pretence of seeking advice on a wide range of subjects. His true aim was to see who would follow him to Alba to fight the combined armies of Olaf Guthfrithson who, it was thought, would sail his massive fleet from Eire into the estuary of the Abhainn Chluaidh at any time. Maerse Guthfrithson's intentions, or so our spies informed us, was to join forces with his father-in-law Constantine II, King of Alba and Owen, the King of Strath Clota. Unless Æthelstan gained full support from the other Saxon kingdoms, he knew Wessex and Mercia would be at the mercy of the enemy's combined force, but that support, at first, didn't appear to be forthcoming. The east coast kingdoms of East Seaxna Rice and East Angles had more than their fair share of Viking blood within their ancestry. It would be difficult to overcome their bias, but Ceint and Suth-Seaxe looked favourably in Æthelstan's direction.

The room was hushed when Æthelstan stood from the dais. He asked one simple question to which nobody knew the answer. 'Why in God's name do they provoke us now?'

His guests remained deadly silent as they looked at each other, open-mouthed in astonishment. For what seemed an eternity, Æthelstan waited for a response, before deciding to continue with his pre-arranged speech.

'If you don't know I shall tell you. They know they can only defeat us if we Saxons are disunited, and that I will march to battle to meet them on the ground of their choosing. If we stay united, we will be victorious, of that I am certain. I will raise my banner in the ground of Englaland, not Wessex or Mercia, or Suth-Seaxe or any other kingdom within our fairest island. I will fight for Englaland but, if my neighbours refuse to fight, then Englaland will never become achievable. It will remain a dream, for I have glimpsed through their veil of deceit. If they wish to suck me into their trap and spit me out without your help, then that is exactly what will happen.

'After my bones are crushed on whatever blood-soaked, mud-caked field in Alba or Ceaster or whatever field they choose, they will not stop there. They will march south until every inch of Saxon land is red with Saxon blood. Our dream of Englaland will be forever lost and Daneland will become a new country on the map of Europe. This I foresee, and so do you. It's up to you, my friends. Join me and see off these heathens forever, or remain behind in your beds like frightened children, hiding beneath your mothers' apron skirts.'

I looked at Æthelstan in disbelief. He was talking to them as if they were children being scolded.

'I fight for the right for every Saxon child to grow to be men. So - are you with me, or do you stay at home to shit in your beds?'

Again, I couldn't believe the way Æthelstan was chastising his fellow Saxon kings, princes, ealdormen and oath-takers to see if any of them would take the bait. There were a few waiverers but those with substantial Danish blood refused to budge until Æthelstan picked up his dragon banner, marched outside and planted it beside the entrance to Maeldunesburh Abbey. When Æthelstan turned around everyone was standing with him.

I knew this was a symbolic gesture, but it was his speech that won the over the faint-hearted. It overflowed with passion, anger, fervour and rage. His words were like a song sung loudly, touching the hearts of all who listened. The symbolic planting of his banner in Saxon soil was the climax, and what a climax it was.

As we walked back inside the abbey, he winked at me as though he had gambled his crown on the wager. I was happy for my king, for he had played his cards close to his chest and won the contest.

'Far and wide things aren't good, said the one who was heard wailing in hell.' I didn't fully understand his proverb, but it made sense in a way.

Æthelstan returned to his seat on the dais with his half-brothers, Ælfweard, Edwin and Edmund alongside him. Once his guests were again seated, Æthelstan addressed them further, as if the forthcoming battle was already won. 'Let's talk tactics.'

Æthelstan was confident that his battle plans were sound and that they would be supported. 'I propose we march north in four separate columns.' He pointed to a map of the British Isles laid upon the floor. 'The first three columns will march in parallel formation with a much larger force about two hours in the rear. The front columns will head north from their respective kingdoms. This way we will confuse the enemy, for you can bet next year's harvest that their spies are already out there scouting our northern borders.' Æthelstan again pointed to the map with his sword. 'Edwin will march north along the border with the unruly Welsh until they reach Ceaster, I will take the middle column and march up the middle lands, whilst our friends from Sussex, Cent and Essex will march up the east coast until...'

Edwin jumped to his feet and interrupted his half-brother, criticising the strategy. Despite Æthelstan's attempts to silence his kin, Edwin continued to voice his contempt.

'Your plan is bound to fail! You have not thought it through. At this very moment our enemies are sure to know of your idiotic plans, and they will slaughter all of us. I cannot - indeed, I will not back you!'

Æthelstan and Edmund were devastated. Their own kin had poured scorn on their jointly agreed strategy and some of the onlookers began to waiver. If the king's own brother rejected the Saxon's battle orders against Olaf Guthfrithson and his northern allies, all looked doomed to failure.

'We must stay united!' he shouted, but Edwin was defiant in his scorn. Æthelstan and Edmund remained seated as honour and custom dictated, but their tempestuous half-brother remained insolent and quickly vacated the Witan.

Æthelstan could not believe Edwin's attitude. All his hard work to achieve unity had flown out the window like the storks in winter. All his plans had come undone in a single brash moment of disagreement, and Edwin had probably lost the lives of thousands of Saxon warriors through his childish outburst. Æthelstan and Edmund had to act. They couldn't leave things as they were, as that would make them look small in others' eyes.

Æthelstan, with Edmund's backing, shouted after Edwin. 'You are excluded and expelled from this court and this Witan forthwith. Find yourself passage to Francia or some other European coastline to contemplate what you have done. When you have calmed yourself down, we might find it in our hearts to forgive you, but not now. Leave us! You are banished!'

Æthelstan and his brothers were deeply shocked and embarrassed. They were angry at Edwin's behaviour. If anyone had the last word, it should be Æthelstan, King of Wessex.

Once calm again, Æthelstan addressed the Witan, but not before he apologised to his brothers regarding Edwin's disruptive outburst. They remained alongside their king to offer their joint support. Edmund moved nearer to Æthelstan's chair and softly whispered a reminder in his ear.

It was obvious to me what Edmund was quietly saying, and our king nodded his acknowledgement.

'Thank you, Edmund. Before we dance with our Viking friends, my brothers and I wish to give voice to our thoughts concerning charters, charges and laws, to be put in place prior to our march north. These ideas are not new. Indeed, my grandfather Alfred had hoped to implement them a long time ago.'

Edmund and Ælfweard nodded their agreement, for they knew of what Æthelstan proposed.

'These charges will be for the benefit and guidance of all our people, every man, woman and child.'

That got the Witan's attention, and I realised that this was where I needed to play the spy, in order to judge who might be for or against any changes in the laws of Saxon Briton. Everyone shuffled uneasily on their feet as they stood and strained to make sure they heard what the king proposed.

Æthelstan then stood up. He appeared taller than usual and his face wore a regal expression of truth and seriousness. He spoke about his new age of living, fair conduct and chivalry.

'Moses,' he told them, 'had Ten Commandments given to him by the hand of God. The Almighty has, however, deemed it inappropriate to give us any, but I have nine proposals I wish to reveal to you. Consider them carefully. We can discuss them when we next meet.'

I was pleased. At least our king was talking in the future tense, so must have thought that there would be another meeting of the Witan. He continued.

'At present these are just basic proposals. We can have them drafted by our scribes for either agreement or disagreement. After all, you are my loyalist supporters and it is only right that you should be the first to hear these proposals. Don't look alarmed, for there is nothing within them that God himself would not see fit to put before this Christian Nation.'

'Well done, my Lord,' I whispered to myself. 'Make it look like divine inspiration has shown itself to God's community in Briton and they will be eating out of your hand before nightfall.'

This proved to be the case. Not a soul opposed the descendants of Alfred the Great, even if Æthelstan cringed at the uttering of the word 'Great'. It was only when they shouted 'Æthelstan the Glorious!' that our king blushed with embarrassment.

The call became a battle song! The Witan kept shouting the phrase, over and over:

'Æthelstan the Glorious! Æthelstan the Glorious!'

They banged their ceremonial shields with their fists as their cries reached new heights. If swords or axes were allowed inside the Witan the roar would have been far louder, but the noise continued unabated until Æthelstan raised his hands, asking them to be silent. With a click of his fingers, Æthelstan ordered the food and drink to be brought into the Witan.

'Let us rejoice in the glorious battle soon to be won!'

I will write of these proposals later, but the news of an unexpected death subdued we Saxons.

Ten days after the Witan disbanded, Æthelstan's heart was greatly broken. Edwin had found a way to have the final word when his body was washed ashore on the Frankish coast.

The flag of Wessex

Chapter 8
Æthelstan's Indecision

It stands now in the track of the beloved multitude,
a wall wonderfully tall, mottled with serpents;
the force of ashen spears has seized its noblemen,
weapons greedy for slaughter.

The well-known way of the world,
and the storms beat against these stony cliffs.
The tumbling snows bind up the earth.

The clash of winter, when the darkness comes.
The night-shadows grow dark,
sent down from the north,
the ferocious hail-showers, in hatred of men.

I always knew when Æthelstan had something on his mind. Again, my senses proved correct, but this time he had numerous problems swimming in his head.

He had concerns about his underlings when they called him 'pretty boy', or 'handsome beautiful boy'. Why this bothered him I couldn't understand, but he told me during one unguarded moment that warriors would only follow a mature, scarred veteran or an experienced mighty leader. Æthelstan might not have had cuts and scars, but his stature and height amply made up for his relative inexperience. I told him that the men of Mercia and Wessex would follow him to the ends of the world if he gave such a command. 'God has protected you from harm.'

He begrudgingly accepted my thoughts on the matter, but he remained troubled by his tormented visions. He put his trust in God, and that trust, since the day of his coronation, had always been positively answered. Æthelstan prayed at least four or five times a day within his private chapel at Malmesbury. Whether God answered him or not I could not ascertain, but he always returned with a pious smile on his handsome face.

He spoke to me of another of his troubles.

'I fear this forthcoming war against the alliance of Irish, Alba and Strath Clota will be unlike any other battle previously fought within this fair land. It will be a battle to end all battles and many will be slaughtered or maimed. There will be insufficient time to bury the dead, just like Byrithnoth's undoing at Maldon in 891.'

I told Æthelstan, in no uncertain manner, that Britnoth, the Lord of Northanhymbre, was undoubtedly a brave warrior and leader of men, but his second-in-command Bishop Ælfwine displayed pure madness when he encouraged his warriors to avenge the death of Byrthnoth. Intelligence and prior surveillance should have won the day, but his pride superseded sound tactics and bravery. He should have withdrawn in good order after witnessing his Lord killed on the battlefield, for it is surely better to fight again another day on different ground than fight a losing battle. The aged Britnoth was already mortally wounded when he received a second blow but, thankfully, he suffered no further punishment.

Byrhtnoth was valiant but not particularly gifted when it came to strategy. He should have kept the Vikings in the fonder Island, for this was far better from a tactical standpoint as it would have penned them in and utilized the waterway as a barrier to our mainland. He failed to do this, however, and thus enabled the Vikings to come across the waterway and battle us on this side, making it far harder for us Saxons to dislodge them once they had built their foundations. Nonetheless, Byrhtnoth was a hero to his warriors, and should be recorded within the chronicles.

Æthelstan considered for a moment then spoke gently with sincere reverence. 'God speedily received his soul.'

Æthelstan recalled the tale of Godric, the son of Ethelgar. He was a brave warrior and a rare man of valour. He was last seen outnumbered and disappearing into a crowd of Viking warriors. 'He was prepared to sacrifice his own life in defence of his King and future country.'

A tear rolled down Æthelstan's pale handsome cheek as he recalled the tales written about the battle at Maldon and the ferocious encounter where brave Saxon warriors were slaughtered in great numbers by the heathen Viking horde. May they rot in hell! Æthelstan then spoke of another Godric, the cowardly son of Odda who, besides being a coward, proved to be a thief and a deserter. He was afraid to fight alongside his men and chose to flee the battlefield, boldly stealing Byrhtnoth's horse to hasten his getaway. His action was a terrible blow to the Saxon warriors, and his cowardly act severely demotivated those under his command.

The Saxons looked for a leader to hold them fast and regroup against the Viking onslaught. Some came to stand in front of the shield wall, among them Offa, Leofsunn and Dunnere, all of whom became fully aware of the plight as the Saxon's swords become fewer. Offa died on the battlefield with his household warriors. The ground changed from bright green to blood red as the day wore on and the causalities grew on both sides. Grown men cried for their wives and mothers, and many were put out of their misery by those bold enough to carry out their gruesome duties. It was better for a friend to speedily send them to heaven than have a Viking push his knife through their eye or slit their throat. By nightfall, on the banks of the River Panta, near Maldon, bodies were piled up, side by side and atop each other, sometimes four or five high. Horses were left with their bellies sliced open, and it was impossible to differentiate between Saxon and Dane, friend or foe. Men on both sides who survived unscathed openly wept at the site of carnage. The fight had gone out of every man still standing alive. Take my word for it, Alder, there were few men left standing. I could not send men to battle with death surrounding my prayers, for war is futile. I wish the Vikings could understand this, but I fear such an ending awaits either them or us at Brunamburh.'

I understood then exactly what concerned Æthelstan so deeply. He feared not for himself but for the good and safe return of his men. He wanted a victory and not a bloodbath, but not a victory at any cost. How he wished that his enemies would accept peace, but there had been too many false hopes of peace already and the Danes had always broken such agreements. The Dane must learn to accept our laws and religion and leave their Pagan past to history. There is only one God, not a God for every day of the week. A God for war, a God for peace, a God for thunder and Gods for the sun and moon. We must not lose sight of the fact that the Danes expressed treason for calling Jesus Christ the nailed God. This is simply an unforgiveable jibe.

My King spoke of a new idea.

'Alder, I have a big favour to ask of you. I wish you to attend this forthcoming battle for I need someone I can trust, and someone who might organise scouting missions. I need eyes and ears in the enemy camps, but what is more I need a man steady of nerve to tell me how many ships are likely to sail from Dublin to our shores and where that landing might take place.'

I suggested that the likely landing shore would be within the Merse, although that might be too obvious a place to beach their ships.

'This is very similar to a game of chess,' he said with an air of uncertainty, 'a case of double-guessing or second-guessing the enemy. I have struggled with making decisions and always second guess myself. Only recently I had to make a choice over something and gave the matter a lot of thought. Months later, however, I still wonder if I made the right one and I can't stop thinking about it.'

I looked at Æthelstan and wondered to what decision he was referring. All I could think of was his banishment of Edwin who, because of Æthelstan's actions, had met an untimely and lonely death, his body washed ashore on some Frankish coast.

Although Æthelstan tried to conceal his torment, it seemed to me that Edwin's death had troubled his mind greatly. Æthelstan eventually came out of his trance-like daydream, however, and spoke to me as a big brother and a friend, no longer King and scribe. 'Good decisions come from experience, and experience comes from bad decisions.'

I turned to look at Æthelstan and tried to make sense of his last remark. The king noticed my look of confusion, put his hands on my shoulders and offered reassurance. 'Don't worry, Alder. I sometimes fail to make sense of my true feelings, but always that I have God on my side and will always put my faith in his hands. Christianity will prevail over the evil pagans, but it pains me when our fellow Saxons fight alongside the Danes and Scots in Northanhymbre.'

'These problems are distracting me from what I promised at the last gathering of the Witan,' Æthelstan continued. 'The need for lawful charters is paramount in my mind and before we march north, we must agree on the wording. Have you had any replies from our allies?'

I told Æthelstan that some had been received and that most of them appeared to be favourable to his suggestions.

Æthelstan suggested I should draw up draft charters for consideration. He wanted the matter finalised before his forces left the safety of the south to do battle somewhere of his enemies' making.

'Don't forget, Alder, I want you to ride with me. If we are victorious, my chronicles must be accurate. If we are to be defeated, then it does not matter for our Englaland will be lost along with our Saxon history.

'We had to teach those men of Alba a lesson two years ago, breaking oaths and stealing our cattle. Now it appears they need to be taught a vital lesson but this time it will be difficult. They have joined forces with the damn Irish, and the forces of Alba and Strath Clota have come together in an unlikely alliance to try and inflict a heavy defeat on me. Well, I say let them try.'

I knew of the incursion into Alba in 934 when Æthelstan invaded Constantine's homeland. He kept his reasons for the invasion to himself and even I was not privy to his decision. The death of his half-brother Edwin in the previous year might have finally removed factions in Wessex opposed to Æthelstan's rule. Guthfrith, the Norse king of Dublin who had briefly ruled Northumbria, died in 934, and any resulting insecurity among the

Danes would have given Æthelstan an opportunity to stamp his authority on the north. I read a chronicle by Clonmacnoise, recording the death in 934 of Ealdred of Bamburgh, which might have given another explanation for the invasion. I knew of a dispute between Æthelstan and Constantine over territorial control instigated by Constantine constantly breaking his oath and his treaty with Æthelstan.

Æthelstan set out on his campaign in May 934, accompanied by four Welsh kings - Hywel Dda of Deheubarth, Idwal Foel of Gwynedd, Morgan AP Owain of Gwent, and Tewdwr AP Griffri of Brycheiniog. His retinue also included eighteen bishops and thirteen earls, six of whom were Danes from eastern England. By late June or early July he had reached Chester-le-Street, where he made generous gifts to the tomb of St Cuthbert, including a stole and maniple, originally commissioned by his step-mother Ælfflæd as a gift to Bishop Frithestan of Winchester. The invasion was launched by land and sea. The Saxon land forces ravaged as far as Dunnottar in north-east Scotland, and the fleet raided Caithness, in the Orkneys.

Although no battles were recorded during the campaign, by September he was back in the south of England at Buckingham, where Constantine witnessed a charter of subregulus, although he acknowledged Æthelstan as his overlordship. During the following year a charter was attested to by Constantine, Owain of Strath Clota, Hywel Dda, Idwal Foel, and Morgan AP Owain.

At Yuletide during the same year, Owain of Strath Clota was once more at Æthelstan's court along with the Welsh kings, but Constantine failed to attend.

I suspect Constantine's absence humiliated Æthelstan to such an extent that it led to a declaration of war. Certainly, Æthelstan was likened to the wolf as opposed to the dove, but the joy of peace had long left our land and we were living in the time of the hated wolf.

The wolf had virtually become extinct within our lands, but it was still classed as an adversary to us Saxons. Our principle adversaries are the devilish Danes, which is why we refer to them in our proverb, 'The wolf must be in the woods, wretched and solitary, whereas a good man should labour for glory in his native land'. We refer to them as vicious wolves, using the name 'wulfheafod' or 'caput lupinum', meaning wolf's head. Wolves, like Danes, could be killed as they were excluded from the laws of man, and lawfully slain by anyone without fear of retribution. It was lawful to drive a Dane or a wolf into the wilderness where they forfeit any legal protection.

We Saxons likened Æthelstan to a dove and Bishop Aldhelm himself always referred to this bird as one representing peace. In ancient Greek myth,

Aphrodite was often depicted with doves because she brought love, beauty and peace, and the dove was the symbolic bird of Athena because it represented the renewal of life. Noah released a dove from the ark which, unlike the raven, returned safely to Noah as proof that the waters were abating. I loved to listen to Bishop Aldhem's stories about the wrath of God pouring down waters on the heads of the pagans, whilst we Saxons, like Noah, were saved from a watery grave.

I was lost in thought when Æthelstan asked how the chronicle was proceeding, to which I naturally answered that everything was in order, detailed and accurate.

'In which case, Alder, before I call another Witan, I wish to make the following declaration. Please write this down exactly as I say:

'I, Athelstan, King of the English, on behalf of myself and my successors, grant to my Burgesses and to their successors of the Burg of Meldufu that they may have and hold always all their tributes and free customs, as they held them in the time of King Edward, my Father, fully and in honour.

'And I enjoin on all beneath my rule that they do no wrong to these Burgesses, and I order that they be free from claims and payment of Scots.

'And I give and grant to them that royal heath land of five hides near my villa of Norton, on account of their assistance in my struggle against the Danes.'

'Proclaiming this has pleased me, and I will sign the declaration this very day. Perhaps I should make clear, however, that I feel that this honour has been taken for granted since my coronation, but it is only rightful I should declare it as the rightful King of the English.

'That marks a good end to the day, Alder, but now I wish you to leave me. Goodnight, my scribe.'

Chapter 9

Laws & Charters

All is misery-fraught in the realm of earth;
the work of fortune changes the world under the heavens.

Here wealth is loaned. Her friends are loaned.
Here man is loaned. Her family is loaned
and this whole foundation of the earth wastes away!

So spoke the wise man in his mind,
as he sat apart in secret consultation.

A good man who keeps his troth
ought never manifest his miseries
too quickly from his breast,
unless he knows his balm beforehand,
an earl practicing his courage.

It will be well for him who seeks the favour,
the comfort from our father in heaven,
where a fortress stands for us all.

Anglo-Saxon poem on Almsgiving

It will be well for that earl who keeps inside himself,
the right-thinking man, a roomy heart,
so that the most of honourable intentions
will be the greatest glory for the world and for our Lord.
Even so this man extinguishes
the flame with the welling waters,
so that he cannot for long be injured
in the cities with the burning brightness
so he with almsdeeds shoves away entirely
the wounds of sinfulness, healing the soul

'I am greatly concerned regarding the disputes between the stone masons within Wessex, Mercia and Eoferwic, Alder. It appears we have no standard practice of payment. Before things get completely out of hand, we must attempt to establish a standard form of recompense for their highly skilled labour. There is even talk of the masons forming guilds between themselves.'

In answer to my king's concern, I enquired how the system worked when the Minster at Eoferwic was built. 'Surely there must have been peace and harmony within the stone mason community when King Edwin of Northanhymbre was baptised there? I well remember Bishop Aldhelm talking about it when I was a young boy.'

'You must remember that we lived differently in those times. The original Minster was a basic wooden structure, not like the magnificent stone building you recall. That was completed in 637 by Oswald who dedicated the Minster to Saint Peter. We have learnt much from the past, Alder. Due to poor standards, the church soon fell into disrepair and was dilapidated in merely thirty years when Saint Wilfrid ascended to the See of Eoferwic. He repaired and renewed the old stone structure and, what is more, he established a school and library within the perimeters of the church grounds. By the eighth century it was among the best and most elaborate structures in Northern Europe.'

'So, what went wrong?' I enquired.

'Even in those days our stone masons could not agree on the criteria with regards to their workmanship. Also, there was the highly contentious problem as to what charges should apply, both for master builders and their apprentices. Journeymen and freemen were a different matter so, in the interest of keeping all sides calm, my grandfather encouraged mutual trust and common sense to both parties. He held peaceful talks and gradually, over time, agreement was reached on the most essential areas of building. These included castles and churches, but that was nearly forty years ago; I fear that once again the crown will have to intervene by calling upon the Witan to specify which charters should apply and to exemplify standards of work and payment. Of course, standards of personal behaviour will have to stand when dealing with social, religious and patriotic behaviour. I need these problems solved before we march north, before we dance with Guthfrithson and his over-zealous fools from Alba and Strath-Clota.

'I have therefore instructed my brother Edmund to call a council gathering before summer ends. We are not blind to the matter, and it must be recognised that the crown is both fully aware of the discontentment and our willingness to bring about a successful conclusion. We must keep our stone masons with us, for I fear the Dane will continue to be a thorn in our side. If the masons decide it is in their best interest to form independent guilds, I see no reason why this should be detrimental to

Englaland. After all there are many academics and societal groups within their ranks, so I see no reason why they would ever threaten the crown. Perhaps we should encourage them to form themselves into guilds or chapters with a royal patronage at their head.'

I considered Æthelstan's words. They certainly made sense, and, with the encouragement of the king, these propositions should appease the stone masons.

I knew that a mysterious fire destroyed much of the Minster Church in the middle of the eighth century, but whether this was arson, or an act of God sent to punish us, I did not know. What I did know was that the Minster was again rebuilt to be such a glorious edifice that it contained no less than thirty golden altars. Bishop Aldhelm once told me that the new Minster was not solely built by the stone masons and their apprentices alone, saying that it was so magnificent and beautiful that the hand of God must have played a part.

Aldhelm even explained to me that ever since the time of King Offa the Minster was held in great admiration by the Saxon, Dane, Norse and Pagan alike.

He continued to explain that the Church at Eoferwic was always considered something sacred and reverent. Perhaps the ungodly Pagan feared the wrath of our Christian God, so the Minster was held in the highest admiration. One of their pagan kings converted to Christianity and is buried within the crypt at Eoferwic.

Æthelstan looked surprised by my knowledge of Eoferwic, but he surprised me even more with his next comment. 'Alder, you do like the sound of your own voice.'

I must have looked puzzled, because Æthelstan smiled warmly at me, before becoming more serious.

'My scribe, you have my thoughts concerning the stone masons and their apprentices and I leave it to you to use the correct words with sincerity, subtlety and diplomacy. Now we must turn our minds to the plight of the ordinary man in my realm. The tax system must look fair and sustainable if we are to raise a permanent fleet and a standing army. The burhs must be reinforced while others must be constructed. If they look upon me as a just king who is constantly worried by his subjects' concerns, they should respect my fairness. Inform the bishops and the priests that Æthelstan loves his subjects, for that is true. It is also true that I need to protect them, but to achieve this noble goal I must pay a fair wage to our seamen and warriors, for they are there to protect Englaland, both on land and at sea.'

'Sire, I have thought about your plans for the men of your realm and have made notes as to how you might wish to proceed in this matter.'

'Make your proposals known to me, for I leave to head my illustrious army by springtime.'

'I will speak quickly, Sire, and I hope they meet with your approval.

'Firstly, it must be stated that every man should be true to God and Holy Church, and be careful to use neither error nor heresy, but be discreet and wise. Secondly, each should be a true liege man to the sovereign without treason or falsehood and, if they should be made aware of any treasonable act, they must warn either the crown or his council. Next, they should be true to one another and treat each other with respect. They should keep the counsel of their fellows in confidence, either in chamber or councils, and keep them in the ways of brotherhood. True men should not sink into thief hood, and refrain from the company of thieves, remaining true to their lord or master. Men should never call any brother or fellow by any foul name. No-one's wife should ever be taken by another in villainy, and no man should harbour ungodly thoughts towards anyone's daughter or servants which could lead to disworship. They should always pay for their meals and drink wherever they may be, both in their own shire or another. Journeymen or craftsmen must be careful not to do any villainy or slander if in a neighbouring shire.'

'Alder, I wish you to re-word the following laws for the good of my people. These charters from the days of my grandfather and beyond will be the foundation of my new Englaland.

'Of lordless men, to which we have ordained, respecting those lordless men of whom no law can be got, that the kindred be commanded that they domicile him to folk-right, and find him a lord in the folk-mote, and if they then will not or cannot produce him at the term, then be he thenceforth a *'flyma,'* and let him slay him for a thief who can come at him, and whoever after that shall harbour him, let him pay for him according to his *'wer,'* or by it clear himself.

'To those we have ordained, that no man buy any property out of port over the agreed price, but let him buy there within, on the witness of the port-reeve, or of another untying man, or further, on the witness of the reeves at the folk-mote.

'If anyone, when summoned, fails to attend the *'gemot'* thrice, let him pay the king's *'oferhyrnes,'* and let it be announced seven days before the gemot is to be. But if he will not do right, nor pay the *'oferhyrnes,'* then let all the chief men belonging to the burh ride to him, and take all that he has, and put him in both. But if anyone will not ride with his fellows, let him pay the king's *'oferhyrnes.'*

'And let there be named in every reeve's *'manung'* as many men as are known to be unlying, that they may be for witness in every suit. And be the oaths of these untying men according to the worth of the property without election.

'Ordinances which the bishops and reeves belonging to London have ordained and with weds confirmed, among our *'frith-gegildas'* as well eorlish as ceorlish, in addition to the dooms which were fixed at Greatanlea and at Exeter and at Thunresfeld.

'That we count always ten men together, and the chief should direct the nine in each of those duties which we have all ordained; and count afterwards their *'hyndens'* together, and one *'hynden man'* who shall admonish the then for our common benefit, and let these eleven hold the money of the *'hynden,'* and decide what they shall disburse when aught is to pay, and what they shall receive, if money should arise to us at our common suit, and let them also know that every contribution be forthcoming which we have all ordained for our common benefit, after the rate of thirty pence or one ox, so that all be fulfilled which we have ordained in our ordinances and which stands in our agreement.

'That we gather to us once in every month, if we can and have leisure, the *'hynden-men'* and those who direct the tithings, as well with *'bytt-fylling'* as else it may concern us, and know what of our agreement has been executed, and let these twelve men have their reflection together, and feed themselves according as they may deem themselves worthy and deal the remains of the meat for love of God.

'And if it then should happen that any kin be so strong and so great, within land or without land, whether twelve *'hynde'* or *'twy-hynde;'* that they refuse us our right, and stand up in defence of a thief, that we all of us ride thereto with the reeve within whose *'manung'*.

Æthelstan stopped his dictation, which I wrongly assumed meant that his renewed law-making had finished, but he appeared instead to be thinking. He stroked his long blonde hair, which seemed to be a habit of his when considering other matters. 'I suppose we should consider the laws of my grandfather and if renewals are appropriate.'

I suggested to Æthelstan that out of respect and courtesy Alfred's laws should never be forgotten. 'You are a respected man of your own making, Sire. Whilst everyone admired Alfred and his son Edward as learned men, you have taken us many steps closer to gaining knowledge and fulfilment. Maybe all that is necessary for me to write is that the laws of King Alfred and Edward remain unchanged, for it is important that the law of treason is upheld.'

'Repeat to me the law of treason, Alder.'

If anyone plots against the king's life, of himself, or by harbouring of exiles, or of his men, let him be liable with his life and in all that he has, or let him prove himself according to his lord's word.'

'And what about stealing from God's church?'

'If anyone thieve aught in a church, let him pay the angylde, and the wite, such as shall belong to the angylde, and let the hand be struck off with which he did it. If he will redeem the hand, and that be allowed him, let him pay as may belong to his word.'

'Excellent Alder. Is there anything else you consider that warrants amending or have we finished for the day?'

I thought for a moment. I had been writing for hours and my left hand was numb through putting quill to parchment. 'I think it right to reinforce the laws regarding God's servants. They seem to have suffered many attacks since Yuletide.'

'Tell me then, Alder. What did my grandfather, Alfred the Learned, have to say on this matter?'

'If anyone carry off a nun from a minster, without the king's or the bishop's leave, let him pay a hundred and twenty shillings, half to the king, half to the bishop and to the church-hlaford who owns the nun. If she lives longer than he who carried her off, let her not have aught of his property. If she bears a child, let not that have of the property more than the mother. If anyone slays her child, let him pay to the king the maternal kindred's share. To the paternal kindred let their share be given to the church.'

Æthelstan's brain was constantly active. He had clearly spent time considering what his grand finale should be regarding his newly revisited charters and laws. I suggested the following to him in the hope of getting some sleep.   We had been talking for many hours and now the full moon shone bright in the night sky.

'May I suggest something, Sire?'

Æthelstan nodded, awaiting my words.

'To all freemen let these days be given, but not to theow-men and esne-workmen, twelve days at Yule, and the day on which Christ overcome the devil, and the commemoration day of Saint Gregory, and seven days before Ēostre and seven days after, and one day at Saint Peter's tide and Saint Paul's, and in harvest the whole week before Saint Mary-mass, and one day at the celebration of All-Hallows and the four Wednesdays in the four ember weeks. To all the theow-men be given, to those to whom it may be most desirable to give, whatever any man shall give them in God's name, or they at any of their moments may deserve.'

'Excellent, Alder. I must be off to prayer and then to a counsel of war with Edmund and the earls. We must make sure our planned march north is well thought through. I am happy that my laws will be applied in my absence. Alder, you have a week, two at the most, before the Witan is called, but for now you must rest. You have more than enough time and parchment, am I right?'

'Yes, Sire,' I replied.

'Wait Alder, I have something to say to you, and you alone. As a friend I wish to inform you that despite constant advice from my council to marry and provide Englaland with a rightful and undisputed heir.

I have decided not to marry,' he declared, 'you will recall the arguments and squabbles after the coronation of my grandfather. Controversy boiled over again once Alfred died, even though Edward had the advantage of being the eldest son of the reigning king, his accession was not assured due to the fact that he had two cousins both of whom had strong claims to the throne of Wessex. Æthelhelm and Æthelwold were the living sons of Æthelred, Alfred's older brother and predecessor as king, but they had been quickly passed over because they were too young when their father died.

My father was forever on his guard should a dagger ever be planted in his back. Æthelhelm remained loyal to my father and became the Earl of Wilsætan, until his death in 1898. However how can we forever forget about Æthelwold's treachery; I do not wish a blood feud on my account bringing an innocent child into this ungodly world. The child would be an innocent ætheling, but evil powers would be always at work and I feel sure the child would not reach two or three years before evil intent would gobble him into the God's earth. Æthelstan struck both of his hand on the table aggressively, as if to exaggerate his uncontrolled anger.

Æthelwold may have had the advantage as his mother Wulfthryth witnessed a charter as queen, whereas Edward's mother Ealhswith never had a higher status than king's wife.

Alfred was in a position to give his own son considerable advantages. In his will, he left only a handful of estates to his brother's sons, however the bulk of his property went to Edward, including all his booklands, the land vested in a charter which could be alienated by the holder, as opposed to folkland, which had to pass to heirs of the body in Cent. The Mercian's described my father as holy inferior to Alfred in the cultivation of letters but incomparably more glorious in the power of his rule.

In the year of our Lord 886 in Lundene my grandfather received the formal submission that he alone ruled over all the Saxon nation who were not under subjection to the Danes, and thereafter he adopted the title Anglorum Saxonum rex or King of all the Anglo-Saxons, which he used in all his charters from that day onwards.

Upon Æthelred's death Edward took control of Mercian lands around Lundene and Oxanforda, leaving Æthelflæd as ruler, in name only, of Mercia. As you know Æthelflæd was not crowned as the Queen of Mercia, however she was always known as The Lady of the Mercia, although she had probably acted as the rightful ruler of Mercia for many years during Æthelred's incapacitation during his later years.

Therefore I consider myself married to Englaland and solemnly promise to care for all my people. Your thoughts Alder, as normal, are much appreciated. I was astonished, why had Æthelstan confided in me and not taken advice from his closest and faithful advisors? My half-brothers will reign after my death; they are now of age and are both well prepared for kingship.'

Chapter 10

The Long March North

Anglo-Saxon poem
'The capture of the Five Boroughs'

In this year, King Eadmund, prince of the Angles
the defender of men, came to Mercia,
the dear start of deeds, to separate Derbyshire,
the White Will's-gate and the River Humber,
the broad stream to the sea.

The five boroughs, Ligorcaster and Lincolnshire
and Snottingham, likewise Stanford as well and Derby.
The Danes were there before
under the North-men bowed over by need
in the binding chains of heathen men
for a long time, until he freed them soon.

For his great honour, the shelter or warriors,
the heir of Eadweard, King Eadmund.

'Do you remember, Alder, when I asked you to be my scribe, many years ago? I took you into my private library and showed you my collection of old books, maps and scrolls, most of those books having been written by the Romans. I read and learnt of their ways, including their building methods, but particularly their road building program. I find it hard today to accept that many of their structures have been left to decay and fall into disrepair. We Saxons prefer not to salvage and repair those magnificent edifices, but instead live a basic life, existing like peasants in timber and thatch dwellings. Do you know why this is, Alder?'

I had heard rumours from the old folk, concerning their fear of living in stone buildings but, not wanting to appear an imbecile in front of my king, I told Æthelstan that I had no thoughts or ideas on the matter.

'You are a bad liar, Alder! I can see right through your dishonesty. I understand the true reasons behind your deceitfulness, however, so I will tell you the reason. They believe the ghosts of Romans walk within those buildings at night, but the truth is much simpler than those silly old wives' tales.

'Quarrying stone is difficult especially when we only have tools with wooden wedges. In addition, transporting stone is extremely difficult when conveying materials on muddy paths, and we have only a few paved roads. Stone buildings are thus very expensive and need large amounts of organised labour. Most of our people are farmers, living off the land, so we have little use of substantial mansions and coloured floors. We are tough people and a fire at night is all we need, not like the Romans with their funny pipes flowing with hot water to keep them warm in their beds. Mud bricks are useless in a country where it rains a lot and fired clay bricks need large amounts of fuel for the furnaces, which again are expensive. Large pieces of stone are heavy and difficult to transport.

'Trees, on the other hand, grow everywhere in our climate. They're easy to cut down and slice into planks. Timber and thatch is plentiful and readily available throughout the kingdom as a building material. Our forests cover most of the landscape except where we have cleared the trees to create homesteads for farming.

However, I am truly thankful to our Roman ancestors for building such impressive straight roads. Consider the skill in building them, Alder, for instead of going around a hill they go over it. The Romans, at one time, might have believed in more than one God but they gradually saw the light of Jesus Christ. Even the Bishop of Christ resides in Rome. It is my intention to convert every soul in Englaland to Christianity. There is no room for Paganism because at the end of this month, after Brunanburh, we will complete our pious challenge by killing or converting the Pagans, for I have given God my oath and kissed the Lance of Destiny.'

I was caught off-guard by Æthelstan's last words. 'What is the Lance of Destiny, sire?' I asked.

'It is the most sacred relic in Christendom, Alder, the lance of Longinus that relieved Christ from his suffering on the cross.'

I wondered aloud why he was reminiscing about the Romans and their buildings and gently questioned the relevance of the conversation.

Æthelstan replied that, as his army would be marching north along the Great North Road in the morning, the discussion was highly relevant. His plan was to have scout outriders about a mile in advance of his main force, thereby able to continually update his commanders. The Aetheling Edmund would march on his left flank and the Bishop of Sherborne would accompany his younger brother and cousin on the right flank.

Æthelstan retained a sizeable faction of the army about three miles to his rear. Our spies in Dyflin informed the king that the Irish fleet, consisting in excess of six hundred ships, was still in harbour waiting to cross the Irish Sea. The Germanic tribes of the Angles, Saxons, and Jutes began their great migration across what we called the German Ocean.

Our ancestors conquered, displaced, and mixed with the native Celtic population, and for most of the time they lived in harmony until the Viking age which began just before the eighth century. For the next two centuries the Vikings ruled the sea, but that has all but ceased when Æthelstan called for a standard navy to protect our shores, coupled with a substantial paid army to protect and defend our homeland.

In the year of Our Lord 937, the summer months were hot and humid, which at least meant that our supply train would not get bogged down in the mud. The Witan had agreed to Æthelstan's every wish, one consequence of which was that an army of over eight hundred thousand men would march north to confront an unknown enemy alliance of thousands. The exact number remained unknown, but we knew they outnumbered us, and on a battlefield of their choosing. Æthelstan had put his entire trust in God and, even as we marched, the king prayed at least three times a day (and four or five on Sundays). He continued this ritual until his scouts reported that the Vikings had left Dyflin. I couldn't help but be afraid, for thousands of Vikings were about to sail across the sea from Ireland where they would meet up with the Scots and hundreds of Saxons from Northanhymbre. Those treacherous Saxons welcomed the opportunity to slaughter the men of Wessex and Mercians, but we hoped to gain a few thousand men from Cent and a few hundred from East Anglia on our way north. Æthelstan hoped to persuade Saxon men of Eoferwic and loyalists from Northanhymbre to join his crusade to rid our nation of the Northmen.

I wondered if Æthelstan was putting too much faith in God.

As promised Æthelstan departed early the following morning. Hundreds of light cavalry scouts left ahead of our main body of men and, at the very stroke of eight, the three forward columns left Lundene with the balance of his army following on behind the king. The mounted scouts were able to keep the three columns within easy reach of each other, making sure they didn't stray more than ten miles apart. Æthelstan required a continuous stream of orders and counter-orders going backwards and forwards between his columns; intelligence was everything. As we passed the lush pastures of Wessex and Mercia, the farming communities cheered and waved, giving colourful garlands of summer flowers to the Saxon troops. It was a sight to stir the emotions, but we eventually left the farmlands behind, instead marching cautiously through dense forests of oak. As if by magic, the forests occasionally blotted out the sun, darkness and sunlight becoming alternative bed fellows. Æthelstan explained that the dance between darkness and light will always remain, but the stars and the moon will always need the darkness to be seen, he made it clear that the moon always borrowed its light from the sun to be seen in the night sky.

'The darkness will not be worth having without the moon and the stars, so start and end your day with God, and always seek His presence and his daily blessings. My grandfather and father tried to convert the Dane to Christianity with bribery, on the understanding they would be bequeathed good farming land in exchange for converting to the true faith. I was never fully persuaded by this approach but, if Alfred and Edward thought it worthy of consideration, then who am I to disagree? I will certainly try to follow in the footsteps of my distinguished ancestors.'

As we marched north the men were in fine fettle. Some sang songs from the old days, and some looked to the priests to steady their nerves whilst I looked to Æthelstan for inspiration. The scouts reported that Bishop Sherborne's column had only reached Camulodunum, whilst Edmund was making good progress with his western column. He had camped for the night at Cirrenceaster. Meanwhile Æthelstan had already crossed the Great Use at Saint Neots but he was worried, for he still hadn't any news from the Maerse about any ships recently arrived from Dyflin. Surely, he thought, over six hundred ships couldn't just vanish, there had been no calamity reported in the Irish Sea which might sink or delay our enemy's passage.

I suggested Æthelstan put himself into the mind of Olaf Guthfrithson. 'What would you do if you were him?'

Æthelstan pondered the question before answering. He had a slight grin on his face as he gave his reply. 'I would sail north around the outer islands of Alba to possibly increase my forces from Alba's islands, then sail down the east coast of Northanhymbre and land my fleet at either the Tinan or the Humbre. This might mean that Bishop Sherborne might be in danger of engaging the Vikings before our forces are united.'

I could see the strain on Æthelstan's face as he grappled with the possibility of Guthfrithson outwitting him. Æthelstan sent orders for the bishop to slow his progress northwards until accurate reports were forthcoming but, in any event, he should not continue further north than Lindcolne. In addition, Æthelstan suggested that Edmund should march towards Buchestanes. After studying his maps, he pointed to a small village named Snotta with his index finger. 'That seems a decent place to set-up camp.' He seemed pleased with the way his alternative plan was developing and rode on with his housecarl's cantering after him.

I hoped that Æthelstan had guessed right concerning Olaf Guthfrithson's possible beaching point for, if he sailed across the Irish Sea, Guthfrithson could still make landfall in the Maerse, thus leaving Æthelstan's western flank exposed to an attack from the west coast, could this be another game of double guessing.

Æthelstan was worried by the early morning mist. I tried to calm his mood by telling him that if we cannot see the enemy, they will be unable to see us. This didn't lift his mood and it was clear that the king was utterly miserable. His eyes glistened with emotion, but he held his head low. His lips trembles as if he were about to shed a tear, but of course but he never did, at least not in public. He suddenly looked up, drew in a breath of air and turned his face towards me.

'Well, Alder. Should we stay here or break camp and march further north?'

I personally didn't see much point in marching anywhere until accurate intelligence emerged. 'Sire to date you have been victorious in every battle you have fought, and each victory was assured due to you knowing what your enemy was up to. I suggest until you have that intelligence we stay here.'

It was obvious Æthelstan didn't like my advice and knew that he had little option but to wait. He didn't like inactivity, but he nodded his head in agreement having seen the sense in my opinion.

At midday the sun had burnt away most of the mist, leaving a bright sunny day. Æthelstan scanned the horizon for signs of enemy activity when, without warning, his face turned greyish-white and despair was engraved across his features. He described the sensation to me later.

'It felt as if something had reached in and ripped my heart out, thrown it on the ground, stepped on it and then put it back. The pain was deep, agonizing and intense. My heart was mangled beyond recognition and my mind was numb, racing in ever-decreasing circles. I tried to make sense of what I had witnessed but I was unable to, instead wondering if it had really happened. I kept telling myself to wake up, unsure if I could ever use my heart again. It might never heal, and the pain would be almost unbearable. I suddenly realised what Jesus felt as he was nailed to the cross.'

On the horizon, on the hills north of Snotta, a small group of enemy scouts could clearly be seen, deliberately taunting us. Homesteads were ablaze and the smell of death reached us.

Afterwards I told Æthelstan that I felt that my heart had also been wrenched out of me and, as I did so, warm salty tears streamed down my cheeks. I searched my mind for some positive words that might turn Æthelstan's despair into renewed hope, but fresh news could not find a way of achieving recognition of what we had just witnessed.

Firstly, our scouts and skirmishers confirmed that the enemy had only been a raiding party, small in number and only intent on stealing provisions. Secondly, a prisoner declared that Olaf had left Dyflin and hoped to land on the Saxon mainland, news that was music to Æthelstan's ears. The captive wasn't privy to the exact location of the fleet's landing although he did state that the men from Alba were on the move.

Æthelstan immediately dispatched orders to his half-brother and Bishop Sherborne to hasten their march north, sending the message that he would meet them south of the Sheaf River. A renewed sense of optimism was being generated in Æthelstan's mind. Although he had only made minor contact with the Danes, the army was aware of the king's growing confidence.

The march from Snotta to the Sheaf was particularly unremarkable due to the lack of any enemy activity. The forest that surrounded Snotta was extremely dense which made marching in a wide formation very difficult, so we reduced our width to ten men astride. This meant that our column was strung out and our rearguard met with the vanguard of our fourth column. In addition, Edmund had marched in a north-easterly direction and was already at the Sheaf to welcome his half-brother. All we waited for was the men of Cent and whatever had been mustered by Bishop Sherborne whilst marching through the land of the East Angles.

Æthelstan was pleased that his Saxon force, headed by his own Mercians, was more than capable of inflicting a substantial defeat on the Viking and Northanhymbre force that awaited him north of the Humbre. The only thing troubling Æthelstan was the constant darkness within the deep, dark forests that surrounded Snotta. His army had to cope with fallen trees and walk on sun-baked rutted tracks, but they discovered renewed vigour through singing, their voices echoing throughout the thick woodland.

In their own way, the priests had also built up confidence and morals. Every man cheerfully marched in support of their king. They idolised him even though, in their eyes, he had been overshadowed by his grandfather. Alfred and Æthelstan were still held in the highest admiration, because each had the gift of charisma which held every warrior's heart and soul in the palms of their hands. Every great leader can dissect and decipher all inefficiencies within his organisation. These visionary traits were attributed to Alfred and Æthelstan, and to a lesser extent Edward, and they often resulted in critical deliberations, aided by a good dose of luck in their decision making. These men carried their followers along on a tide of goodwill and confidence.

The Saxon army had crossed the Sheaf by means of the Roman stone bridge. They were marching methodically towards the village of Dore in southern Eborakon, where King Egbert of Wessex led his army to the village to receive the submission of King Eanred of Northanhymbre, thereby establishing his overlordship over the whole of Anglo-Saxon Britain. Our numbers swelled to nearly 90,000 warriors as we arrived at the village of Dore. It felt strange, as though we were living outside the rules of normality. A battle had to take place, in which thousands would die, but the Saxons needed to be victorious or the dream of Englaland would be lost forever. If we lost the Danes would sing of their great victory, and how the Saxons ran away from a battle.

'Where is the Bishop of Sherborne and my cousin? They should have arrived by now.' The normally calm Æthelstan was frustrated by Sherborne's absence. 'Have you had any reports, Alder?'

'No sire,' I answered. I spoke the truth - Bishop Sherborne and his men were late. I informed the king that enemy activity had been reported to the north and west of the villages of Soke and Donceaster, and that the area had seen plague but had left the land some years earlier.

'Surely the Danes wouldn't choose this location to fulfil their dreams? To fight on the craggy moors of Eoferwic would be unthinkable to Olaf,' Æthelstan retorted. 'The moorland would certainly not be my first choice for a battle, as I reasoned Olaf Guthfrithson and his Irish and Alba turds would have preferred a completely different location. Somewhere near the sea to assist a retreat, for retreat is what they will most certainly be seeking after we slaughter their best fighters.'

'Alder, inform Edmund and all our commanders that their attendance is required in my tent at midday, for I have policies and strategy to discuss.' Æthelstan tried his best to appear calm and steady as he spoke.

At midday Edmund and the earls had gathered around a makeshift map of the moorland by the banks of the River Don, the only exception being Sherborne, who still hadn't made an appearance. Æthelstan was greatly concerned for the safety of the bishop and ordered his mounted scouts to carry out an intensive search to find out where he had gone.

By the time the sun had set over Donceaster, news came to inform Æthelstan that the bishop had sadly arrived late and had set up his camp beyond enemy lines. The scouts were nervous about telling Æthelstan that Sherborne's column had been massacred, and every Saxon warrior had been slain, stripped of mail, and weapons and rations. 'I have to report that the ravens are feasting on their bodies as we speak,' said one scout.

'Where did this atrocity take place?' Æthelstan demanded to know.

'Oderesfel,' came the reply. This meant that the Danes had crossed the Irish Sea and made landfall in the Maerse, whilst Æthelstan had marched in a north-easterly direction. Olaf had anchored in the Maerse and had slaughtered the Bishop's men at Oderesfel, or had the Danes and Scots split forces to hit us from the Maerse and the Humbre?

'These Danes are pure evil, but I will be avenged!'
Æthelstan shouted.

Æthelstan asked to be left alone while he prayed
for the souls of those killed. He vomited heavily
afterwards but, once his stomach and bowels were
emptied, he returned to the tent flap he stood upright to
shout a defiant declaration towards his unseen enemy.

'There will be no mercy and no quarter given
tomorrow! The enemy are already walking ghosts!' He
ducked his head as he re-entered the tent and prayed for
forgiveness to God, knowing that many men would die by
his sword's edge come the morrow.

Æthelstan requested my company inside his
command tent, the purpose of which quickly became
obvious. 'Alder, there will be no more bloodshed until
Olaf Guthfrithson and myself meet to agree on the
location of the battlefield.'

'I don't follow sire,' I replied.

'As blood thirsty as Guthfrithson was there are
certain rules we have to comply with before a spear can
be thrown, or a sword is drawn in sunlight.'

'Rules, what rules,' I asked, failing to understand a
single word my king was trying to explain.

'Guthfrithson and I must agree with the battles
exact location, we then have to agree on the parameters,

we then have to appoint stewards from both armies to fix hazel sticks into the ground and finally agree a time for the battle to commence.'

'These sickening blood-soaked engagements have very complicated rules, but how can you trust Guthfrithson to abide by the rules?'

Æthelstan thought about my question before answering. 'If he fails to abide by the rules, I will quickly kill him and will make sure everybody knows what a coward he was.'

Chapter 11

'Brunanburh'

The battle to end all battles

(The Great Battle)

In this year, King Æthelstan, lord of earls,
ring-giver of warriors, and his brother as well,
Eadmund ætheling achieved everlasting glory in battle,

with the edges of swords near Brunanburh.
They cleaved the massed shields,
hewed the battle-wood, the relics of hammers,
of the heir of Eadweard,
as it suited their heritage,
so that they often in battle defended their lands,
treasures, and homesteads
against every one of the hateful.

Foemen were felled, the Scottish people,
the ship-sailors fated were destroyed,
the fields grew slickened with the blood of men,

after the sun passed upwards over the earth.
in the morning-time, the remarkable star,
the bright candle of God, the Eternal Lord,
until that noble creation sank to its rest.
There lay many warriors, seized by the spear,
the northern men, over their arrowed shields,
likewise the Scottish also were weary, saddened by war.
The West-Saxons in their ranks rode down
the long day the hateful people,
chopping down the battle-fleers from behind
so sorely with sharply ground swords.

The Mercians did not deny any of those warriors
their hard hand-playing,
those who had sought their land with Olaf
across the blending of oars upon the bosom of the sea,
fated to fighting.

Five young kings lay slain on the battlefield,
put to sleep by the sword,
Likewise, seven more of the earls of Olaf,
and an uncountable army,
their sailors and Scots.
There the lord of the Northmen was put to flight,
driven by need to the stem of his ship,
with but a little army the ship pressed into the water,
the king departed there onto the fallow flood, sparing his spirit.
Likewise, there also the aged man came into the sea
into his northern homeland.

Constantinus, the hoary battle-warrior,
having no need to cry out about the match of his pairing,
his might was slashed,
deprived of his friends upon the folk-stead,
smitten in battle,
and losing his son upon the slaughter-field,
ground down by wounds,
the young man at war.

There was no need to boast for the blond warrior
of the sword-slaying, old and devious,
nor Olaf any more among their battle-leavings
they had no need to laugh
about how they were better in battle-works
upon the fighting-field, under the flaring flags,
at the conclave of spears, the meeting of men,
the exchange of weapons, after they upon the killing-field,
playing against the heir of Eadweard.

Those North-men departed into their nailed barques,
the dreary leavings of the spear upon the Irish Sea
across the deep water, seeking Dublin,
and Ireland abashed in mind.

Likewise those brothers both together,
king and his nobleman, sought that country,
West-Saxon-land, exultant in warfare.
They left them behind to divide up the carrion,
the dusky-plumed fowl, that darkened raven,
horn-beaked and that hazel-feathered eagle,
white behind it, enjoying the slain,
the greedy war-hawk and that grey beast,
the wolf in the wold.

Nor was there a greater slaughter
upon this island ever yet, the people slain
before these edges of swords, of which the books speak,
the elder historians, after the Angles and the Saxons
arrived up from the east hither over the broad sea
seeking Britain, the haughty war-smiths,
overwhelming the Welsh, men eager for glory
obtaining their new homeland.

By the time we arrived at the chosen place Æthelstan's army were soaking wet and tired, even though we felt the cold, I was suddenly aware of a sense of invincibility. It is strange that a battle somehow calms the nerves. In my mind the enemy had little chance of victory because they were too slow and cumbersome. Our two armies faced each other across the open field, hurling taunts and obscenities across the grasslands that would inevitably turn red with fresh blood. Warriors on both sides of the divide crashed their swords or spears on the back of their shields creating as much noise and mayhem as they could.

I kept a close eye on Æthelstan, for he alone seemed utterly confident of the task that lay before him. There was no need for him to shout or scream futile gestures at the combined armies of Irish and Scots. He knew what was expected of his men, for his warriors had been briefed by their commanders. There was no need for any rousing battle speech or to call upon the help and guidance of the Almighty. Æthelstan knew his men were frightened but they were fighting to protect their wives and children - the fight to protect Saxon Englaland came second on their list. We could smell urine and shit in the air as Æthelstan slowly walked his horse along the front rank of his force. Whether he contained his warrior's fears I couldn't tell but it did no harm for his army to view their king so secure and self-assured. He hoped his posture and self-belief would somehow filter down to his men.

This was the calm before the storm. Æthelstan knew that very soon Olaf would signal his bloodthirsty Danes to move forwards, for it was his intention to instil panic and trepidation into the minds of the Saxons. Æthelstan ordered his men to stand firm in the face of the enemy, shouting above the constant din of the clashing shields.

'Men from Englaland you fear no one!'

I must confess I wondered what I, the king's scribe, was doing on what was to become a field of death. I knew that, by nightfall when the sun had passed over the western sky and dropped out of sight, thousands of widows would mourn for their men folk.

The Vikings moved closer to our front rank. We had the slight advantage of higher ground with the trees to our backs, whilst the Dane had the river behind them where some of their long boats were still moored. The noise was continuous and deafening. Æthelstan continued to look cheerful as he paraded astride his horse ahead of his warriors. He smiled as he attempted to speak to his men, deliberating stopping in front of those who appeared anxious about the oncoming battle, trying to contain their terrors.

The enemy had closed the gap between our front ranks to no more than two hundred yards when Olaf Guthfrithson was sighted upon his horse. He cantered ahead of his warriors, gesturing insults as he studied and mirrored Æthelstan's stance. Towards the rear of Guthfrithson's front line his spearmen and archers could clearly be seen readying themselves to act once their commander gave them orders. Æthelstan, aware of the damage Guthfrithson's arrows could inflict, gave the order for a 'shield wall.' His front row lowered their shields to ground level, the second rank covered the torso and the third rank, and those behind, covered the skull. The Saxons had rehearsed the shield wall many times before, so it was soon ready and effective.

To me it looked exactly like a wave crashing down onto the beach. I thought to myself that if I survived this battle, I must include that expression within my chronicle, but first I had to contain my nerves and bowels as it appeared that chaos would surely reign across the battlefield.

The enemy suddenly rushed forwards, smashing themselves against our front rank. Æthelstan was constantly thinking, strategy and tactics always churning in his brain. Our shield wall held as the enemy attempted to push us back. Men began to fall as our best warriors thrust their spears and swords against the enemy.

A man from Srath-Clota ran onto the point of my spear and I felt the impact on my arm as the spear punctured his stomach muscles. His guts and warm blood splattered across my face and, as he screamed, I tasted stale mead on his breath. His body trembled as I tried to free my spear from his belly. I released my spear and punched him in the groin, then thrust my sword into his throat. I watched as his life ebbed away in front of me.

The noise of dying and wounded men encircled my thoughts, but I had no time to think. Everything appeared to be moving at a slower pace than usual. My head was hazy and numb as I thrust my sword into the bare shoulder of a Dane, as he swung an axe at a friend standing close to me in the shield wall. I was horrified to find the enemy was a shield-maiden. It came to my mind that their impulsive attack had not been well thought through, as the enemy continued to rush forward without any thought for their own safety. This was my first time inside a shield wall, and I hoped it would be my last. The stench of stale breath and ale, urine and gore, fear and apprehension heightened the sensations of a living within a kind of hell; my numbness caused my body to act without feeling.

Yet again the shield walls crashed together. Iron struck against wood, spears splintered, and swords were discarded, as both sides fought with an anger I had never previously witnessed. Arrows flew overhead but our shield wall held, whereas the Danes had abandoned their shields. Nothing seemed real anymore, especially when it appeared to rain, but the rain was blood, the spray formed as throats were cut, bellies slashed, and limbs were hacked from the torso. All I could do was try to stay alive and continue killing the terrifying, wide-eyed men with blooded faces who came towards me.

To my mind, Constantine and Guthfrithson were at odds with each other, a point that Æthelstan instantly exploited. It appeared that the fire had left Constantine's belly. His determination to stay and fight had diminished to the extent that he and his men were looking to their rear to find an easy option to withdraw from the field, for they were already beaten and looked solely for self-preservation. The men from Alba were lined up on the right flank of Guthfrithson's men so, if Æthelstan could rapidly break Constantine's forces and compel them to retire from the battlefield, and then others would swiftly follow his example.

They probably considered they could defeat the Saxons by superior numbers alone, but they had not considered Æthelstan's quick brain. The enemy's shield wall was fast disintegrating, the men from Alba were being driven back, and the only thing on their mind was to run. The Saxons were beating the life out of the Scots. The smells of fear and drained bowels were in the air, along with blood, urine and vomit. Broken shields covered the field, and there were limits to where the enemy could run.

The so-called 'Great Battle' had quickly disintegrated into a Viking rout. On the far side of the field our mounted spearmen circled behind the Scots to attack their archers. Constantine and Guthfrithson knew that all was lost. Their futile attempt to slaughter Æthelstan and his Saxon warriors rapidly collapsed into a farce. Mounted Saxon spearmen were ordered to the front to complete their ugly work, and the sound of men screaming filled the air as Scot and Dane fell in their thousands. The warriors from Strath Clota fled with their comrades from Alba, their sole intention being to find a way home before an axe, sword or spear penetrated backbones or splintered skulls. Some reached the border and safety, but thousands suffered an agonising death on the long weary march home. Meanwhile Guthfrithson escaped into the waters and the relative safety of his ships. Due to Guthfrithson's panicking, thousands of Danes never made it back to the sea. No prisoners were taken, and Æthelstan was true to his oath. No quarter or mercy was given to his adversaries, for they had made their choice and paid a great price as the sun disappeared over the western horizon.

The Saxons pursued the Danes and Scots throughout the night, and it was easy to find their way back to Æthelstan's camp. All they had to do was follow the long line of enemy dead.

As the sun smiled on the eastern horizon, Æthelstan and Edmund requested that I walk with them as they surveyed the battlefield. Thousands of men littered the ground at our feet; some piled more than five bodies high. Discarded weapons, mail and helmets were scattered everywhere. We tried to pile them onto carts, but the task was immense, and we simply ran out of places to put them. Those who were too badly wounded were quickly put out of their misery, but there were more Danes than Saxon corpses.

Both Æthelstan and Edmund had their housecarls with them for protection. Not that they were needed, for the invaders were completely broken. We put swords into their hands and wished them a speedy journey to the halls of Valhalla. Some thanked us and smiled, but others were only just clinging to life.

Æthelstan asked me a question. 'Where exactly are we, Alder?'

Neither I nor Edmund knew the location, however I tried to answer. 'I believe they call this meadow Brunanburh.'

'Today this field will be known as the field of death and destruction. Many Christian souls have found their way to heaven and I wish them happiness in the afterlife, but it is truly a sad day. This battle should never have happened, for if only Guthfrithson of Dyflin, Constantine of Alba and Owain of Strath Clota had shown more sense, all this carnage could have been avoided. The ravens, eagles and wolves would have remained hungry for another day, but I have a feeling that men will always fight one another. Come - let us leave this place. The images of warriors with gaping wounds, choking and gurgling on their own blood will stay with me for as long as I live.'

'What should I write of today, Sire?' I asked.

Unlike Edmund, Æthelstan looked downcast and full of grief. He told me to write simply and concisely.

'Write something like this. Æthelstan and Edmund, with their West-Saxons and Mercians, slaughtered the Scots and Norsemen. Constantine and his Scots fled to their homeland in the north. Olaf and what remained of his Norsemen fled across the sea to Dyflin, leaving the corpses to the raven, the eagle and the wolf.'

At sunset I learnt that more than fifty thousand enemy warriors fell on during that day at Brunanburh, and we still perused the enemy throughout the night. Our casualties, although high, were no more than ten thousand. As we began our slow journey home to Mercia and Wessex, the song grew stronger: 'Æthelstan the Glorious!' These three simple words reverberated throughout the day, for indeed Æthelstan was glorious in victory.

Æthelstan the Glorious! Æthelstan the Glorious!

For Æthelstan was indeed glorious in battle.

Viking Warrior

Epilogue

Nothing Lasts

Æthelstan, my friend and king, died on the twenty-seventh day of October in the year of our Lord 939, a mere twenty-seven months after the sickening bloodletting at the great battle of Brunanburh. The king died on one of his estates in Gleawecestre but he demanded not to be buried at the New Minster. Æthelstan had already left clear instructions that he wished to be interred within the confines of Malmesbury Abbey.

Edmund succeeded Æthelstan to the throne of Englaland and, like his brother; he was crowned king at Kingston upon Thames. The coronation took place on the twenty-ninth day of November 939. Edmund ruled over an ever-decreasing kingdom, and his reign was only notable for its constant warfare. He was assassinated whilst attending mass at Pucklechurch in Gleawecestre, less than seven years after his ascension to the throne.

During those six and a half years, Edmund lost most of that which Æthelstan had gained, including lands in the mid-lands, Northanhymbre, Eoferwic and Strath-Clota, all of which returned to Danish rule. Edmund's first wife was Ælfgifu of Shaftesbury. They had two sons from this union - Eadwig (c940-959) and Edgar (c943-975). They both became kings of Englaland. Ælfgifu died in 944 and, following her death, Edmund married the lady Æthelflæd from Damerham in Gleawecestre. There are no known children from this second marriage.

Eadred was crowned King of the English following his brother's assassination. His major achievement during his short reign was to free Northanhymbre from Danish rule when Eadred defeated and expelled the murderous Viking Erik Bloodaxe.

Eadred died at Frome, Sumorsaete, on the twenty-third day of November 955 following a strange sickness of the stomach. Apparently, he had a longstanding illness which prevented him from consuming anything but the juices of his food. Eadred was buried in the Old Minster at Winchester.

I was invited to Eadwig's coronation at Kingston upon Thames which was to be held at the end of January 956. Due to a fever I was unable to attend but was told afterwards that Eadwig had grown bored of the celebrations and retired to his own apartments, even though the coronation feast was in full swing. When Archbishop Oda noticed Eadwig's absence, he sent Abbot Dunstan in search of the errant king. Dunstan supposedly found Eadwig in a compromising situation with a young woman, a girl of ripe age together with her mother. I was informed that Dunstan was so furious he physically attacked both women before dragging Eadwig back to the banquet.

I would have loved to witness Eadwig's fall from grace. It was rumoured that he was constantly at odds with the church. Eadwig died from an inherited illness on the first day of October 959, aged just nineteen years. I often wondered if the cause of this unknown sickness started with Alfred, but I doubt if anyone will ever know.

I have grown old and I look forward to sharing a conversation with my dear friend and king Æthelstan, who united our country and brought Alfred's dream to fruition - a united Englaland. I wonder what the chroniclers of the future will make of my story. Will they marvel at the name of Æthelstan or will they bury this parchment along with his name? I sometimes think to myself they will choose the latter, but I have no real power to prevent Æthelstan becoming a forgotten man, or even a forgotten king.

Alder later wrote that Æthelstan's victory preserved the unity of England.

The fields of Britain have been consolidated into one. We have peace and harmony everywhere, and abundance of all good things. It was the greatest battle in our Anglo-Saxon history. Sadly, I cannot pin-point the sites of the battle other than tell you it was at a place called Brunanburh.

Alder died on Yuletide Eve in the year 960.

The few friends left alive saved him from a pauper's burial and at great expense he was laid to rest, like Æthelstan at Malmesbury Abbey.

Æthelstan's Family Tree

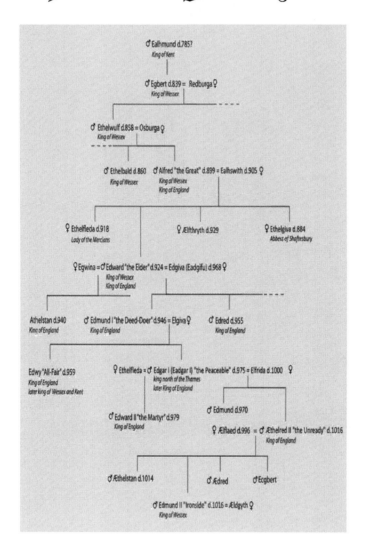

Historical

Notes

Alder/Alander:	Excepting Alder and his father, Alander, every other named character existed together with the battles they fought.
Maeldunesburh:	Malmesbury Abbey, Wiltshire.
Sinistra: left-	From the Latin meaning 'evil or a handed person.
Scireburnan:	Sherborne, Dorset.
Wiltunscir:	Wiltshire, named after the former county town of Wilton.
Sumorsaete:	Somerset.
Durnovaria:	Dorchester in Dorset.
Dumnonia:	Dorset.

West Wealas:	In Anglo-Saxon times the county of Cornwall was known as West Wales.
Alfred the Great: Wessex between	Or King Ælfrēd (in the Anglo-Saxon style) was the King of 871 until 886 and King of the Anglo-Saxons between 886 until his death in 899. He was never classed as the king of the English. Ælfrēd was the youngest son of King Aethelwulf of Wessex. His father died when Ælfrēd was young and three of his brothers reigned before him. Alfred/Ælfrēd was born in Wantage. He married Ealhswith, a descendant of the Royal House of Mercia in the year 868. There were many Anglo-Saxon kings who were considered great military leaders, but what made Alfred stand out is that he was interested in learning, and in the promotion of English as a written language. Alfred was the only king of Wessex to be given the title of 'Great,' although he refused to adopt this title during

his lifetime. It was only during the sixteenth century the Alfred was first called Alfred the Great. (Book 26 of the *'Historiae Anglicae'* by Polydore Virgil published in1534) prior to this date he was simply known as King Alfred of Wessex. Originally, Alfred had no epithet, except *'Alfred the Learned'* as recorded within the Chronicles of Roger of Howden (1174-1201). The reason why he probably started to get singled out was because there was a lot of history about him, due to his life as written by Asser, and because there was a popular set of oral transmission verses known as the 'Proverbs of King Alfred'. These proverbs were well known among the common folk and recited at entertainments, making him a kind of a folk figure.

Northanhymbre: Northumberland.

Venta Caester: A former Roman settlement, best known today as Winchester.

The Seven Heptarchy:	In Anglo-Saxon times it was the name given to the seven separate Saxon kingdoms.
Daneland:	The historical name given to those parts of England held by the Vikings.
Saxons, Angles & Jutes:	The Jutes originated from the Jutland peninsular. The Angles and Saxons were comprised of Germanic tribes, the Saxons originating from the North Sea coast of the Netherlands, Germany and Denmark. Their name is derived from the seax, type of knife popularly used by the tribe. The Angles originated from Angelin, a small district in northern Germany.
Battle of Ethandun:	Otherwise known as the Battle of Edington in Wiltshire. It was fought in the month of May 878, between the Great Heathen Army led by Guthrum and King Alfred, which resulted in an Anglo-Saxon victory.
Humbre:	The River Humber.

Monkceaster:	Refers to Newcastle upon Tyne.
Tinan:	The Anglo-Saxon name for the River Tyne.
King Alfred's illness:	He probably suffered throughout his lifetime with what we call Crohn's disease today.
The Celtic Tanist:	The tanistry is a Gaelic system, notably in Scotland and Ireland for passing on titles and lands.
Burning of the Cakes:	was recorded three hundred years after Alfred's death. It seems unlikely to be true, unless the cakes coincided with the month of February, during which the Anglo-Saxons celebrated with the giving and receiving of cakes.
Oxanforda:	Oxford.
Battle of Aclea: Oak	In the year 851 the West Saxons defeated the Viking raiders at Field, Aclea near Canterbury.
Cantaware:	Canterbury in Kent.

Cent or Cantia:	The county of Kent. The Romans called Kent - Cantium, meaning chalk.
Cornwalum:	Cornwall.
Lunar or Moon months:	The first full moon in a thirteen-month cycle was called a blue moon and the year was referred to as *'þæs monan gear'* or the moon year.
Battle of Englefield:	On New Year's Eve in 871, a battle took place near Reading in Berkshire between the West Saxons and a Viking force. After one of the Viking earls died, the Viking fleet was overthrown. They consequently broke and ran, but the victory was only short-lived.
Berrocshire:	Berkshire.
Battle of Ashdown:	In January 871, the Saxons defeated a Viking invading force. The exact location of Ashdown remains unknown, but some consider Kingstanding Hill to be the likely location.

Battle of Basing:	At the end of January 871 the Danes defeated a West Saxon force at Basing, Hampshire.
The Battle of Merton:	The battle took place in March 871 within Wessex borders. The actual site of the battle remains unknown, but the likely locations are Dorset, Hampshire or Wiltshire. The outcome of the battle first appeared to favour a Saxon victory over the Great Heathen Army, but the Danes, having split their army in two, remained masters of the field. See also the battle of Maldon (a separate battle, with a similar name).
Readingum:	Reading in Berkshire.
Hamtunscir:	Hampshire.
Hamptunr:	Southampton Waters.
Fulanhamme:	Fulham.
Lundene:	London.
Temes:	The River Thames.

Battle of Buttington: In 893, in the county of Kent a Viking army fought an allied force of Anglo-Saxons and the Welsh. Victory that day belonged to the Anglo-Saxon/Welsh force.

Bemfleot: Benfleet in Essex.

Battle of Holme: This took place on 13th December 902 when a Wessex/Kent force fought the East Anglian Danes lead by the Saxon Æthelwold and Eohric the Dane. The course of the battle and its exact location is unknown, but Holme in Huntingdon seems likely. As for the victor, it appears both armies retreated in good order, but Æthelwold and Eohric were both slain, thus ending Æthelwold's revolt.

Wulfruna's town on the great hill Tettenhall, Wolverhampton:

     Wulfruna was a Saxon noble woman. She inherited her lands from King Edmund (Æthelstan's brother and successor).

Wulfruna lived at a time of Mercian dominance. She was imprisoned by Olaf Guthfrithson at Tamworth. The Battle at Tettenhall was a turning point in the wars against the Danes.

River Saefern:	River Severn, or River Lode.
The Nephilim:	According to the book of Genesis, the Nephilims were the offspring of the sons of God and the daughters of men.
Ceaster:	Chester.
Dyflin:	Dublin.
Eoferwic:	The City of York or, as the Danes knew it, Jorvik.
Deor or Dore:	A village in South Yorkshire.
Derbentio or Deoraby: the	Known today as Little Chester on outskirts of Derby.
Ledecestre:	Leicestershire.
A Hide:	In Anglo-Saxon times, a hide related to a measurement of land deemed sufficient to support a family. Today a hide would be

equivalent to approximately 30 acres. A hide was not a constant measurement as it related to the quality of the soil. The hide was common throughout England, except in Kent, where the term 'weald' was used. In Yorkshire the term riding was used.

Alba: Scotland.

Bebbanburg: Bamburgh, Northumberland.

Coria or Corbridge: An old Roman fort, two miles south of Hadrian's Wall in Northumberland. Bloody Acres is reputed to be the location of the Battle of Coria which took place around the year 914.

Strath-Clota: Strathclyde, Scotland.

Yuletide: Christmas.

Englaland: England.

Hacmunderness: a town in north-west Lancashire.

Abhainn Chluaidh: The Irish name for the Mersey estuary.

Suth-Seaxe: Sussex.

Æthelstan's argument with Edwin:

> Never took place. It was convenient for me to show that, although the brothers were at odds, I had to clear Æthelstan from any involvement in Edwin's death.

Æthelstan's rousing speech at the Witan:

> Again, never took place, but it seems reasonable to suggest that this would be type of battle cry he would deliver.

Æthelstan the Glorious: Æthelstan was later known by this name, but not until after the Battle at Brunanburh.

The battle of Maldon: as opposed to the battle of Merton, took place by the banks of the Planta, Essex. This extract is from James Garnett's excellent book, published in 1900.

Byrhtnoth: *'and his East-Saxons are drawn up on the bank of the Planta. The wikings' (sic) herald demands tribute. Byrhtnoth angrily offers*

arms for tribute. Wulfstan
defends the bridge. Byrhtnoth
proudly permits the wikings (sic)
to cross. The fight rages.
Byrhtnoth is wounded. He slays
the foe. He is wounded again. He
prays to God to receive his soul,
and is hewn down by the
heathen men. Godric flees on
Byrhtnoth's horse. His brothers
follow him. Ælfwine encourages
the men to avenge the death of
their lord. So does Offa, who
curses Godric. Leofsunn will
avenge his lord or perish.
Dunnere also. Others follow their
example. Offa is slain and many
warriors. The fight still rages. The
aged Byrhtwold exhorts them to
be braver as they become fewer.
So does Godric, not he who fled.'

Payment of Scot: refers to an assessment of tax.

Æthelstan owned land in Foxley in what is now Wiltshire, and gave the nearby town of Malmesbury 600 acres of land. To this day, the land is still

	owned by the Freemen of the town.
Fine fettle:	If you say that someone or something is in fine fettle, you mean that they are in very good health or condition.
Camulodunum:	Colchester in Essex.
The Use:	The River Ouse, Huntingdon.
Lindcolne:	Lincoln in Lincolnshire.
Buchestanes:	Buxton in Derbyshire.
Brunanburh:	Where was *Brunanburh*?
	Where was the stretch of water called *dinges mere* – mentioned in the Brunanburh poem – if indeed this is a place name at all?
	Many theories have been put forward to answer these questions, but none have thus far solved the mystery. Bromborough on the Wirral peninsula is often promoted as the best candidate for the site, primarily because it was originally recorded as

Bruneburgh and *Brunburg* in a twelfth-century document.

The place-name dispute for Bromborough is certainly strong, but it is by no means decisive. Even if it was once known as *Brunanburh*, there is no certainty that the great battle of 937 was fought nearby, for we have no reason to assume *Brunanburh* was a unique place-name in Anglo-Saxon England. There might have been several places so named in different areas, with not all of them being identifiable today in their modernised forms. It is also worth considering the position of Bromborough, relative to Scotland. Why would a combined force of Scots and Strathclyders choose to fight a battle there? If these northerners wanted to raid Athelstan's territory and challenge him to a showdown, they could achieve both objectives without marching so far south. Personally I am convinced that Olaf Guthfrithson beached his ships in the Maerse. The Viking leader was no idiot. In case the battle went ill he needed an easy escape route back to Ireland and Doncaster (lately named as a possible site for Brunanburh) does not fit the criteria. The Saxon Brunanburh poem mentions the Irish Sea from whence Guthfrithson left the mainland once the battle was lost, leaving the dead to be devoured of by the ravens, sea-eagles and wolves. I remain confident that Bromborough was formerly known as Brunanburh mainly because Doncaster was too far away from the west coast of England. Had Æthelstan been defeated it would have been the end of Anglo-Saxon England. However upon victory Britain was created for the first time and Æthelstan became the de facto king of all Britain, the first in its history.

The battle of Brunanburh is mentioned or alluded to in over forty Anglo-Saxon, Irish, Welsh, Scottish, Norman and Norse medieval texts.

One of the earliest and most informative sources is the Old English poem *Battle of Brunanburh* in the Anglo-Saxon

Chronicle, which was written within two decades of the battle. The poem relates that Æthelstan and Edmund's army of West Saxons and Mercians fought at Brunanburh against the Vikings under Anlaf (i.e. Olaf Guthfrithson) and the Scots under Constantine. After a fierce battle lasting all day, five young kings, seven of Anlaf/Olaf's earls, and countless others were killed in the greatest slaughter since the Anglo-Saxon invasions. Olaf and a small band of men escaped by ship over Dingesmere to Dublin. Constantine's son was killed, and Constantine fled home.

Wendune:

Where was *Wendune*, another place associated with the battle, which interestingly states that in the year 937 of the Lord's Nativity, at Wendune which is called by another name Brunnanwerc or Brunnanbyrig, Æthelstan fought against Olaf/Anlaf, son of the former king Guthfrith, who came with 615 ships and had with him the help of the Scots and the Cumbrians. The account continues..... Olaf/Anlaf, the pagan king of the Irish and many other islands, incited by his father-in-law Constantine, king of the Scots, entered the mouth of the River Humber with a strong fleet.

But what was that important to point a finger at Wendune? First, the suffix *'dune or dun'* in Anglo-Saxon times was an adjective meaning - dull greyish-brown coloured. The prefix *'Wen'* makes little sense unless you look for a dull greyish-brown river north of the Humber in Yorkshire.
The River Went is a river in Yorkshire, England. It rises close to Featherstone and flows eastward, joining the River Don at Reedholme Common.

Therefore I pose the question, could Reedholme Common be the site of the great battle of Brunanburh.

Snotta: The small village named after Snotta, today known as Nottingham.

The Sheaf: A river in Sheffield.

Eborakon:	The Anglo-Saxon name for the village of Dore in South Yorkshire.
Oderesfel:	Huddersfield.
German Ocean:	Former name of the North Sea.
Olaf Guthfrithson:	Sometimes referred to as Anlaf Guthfrithson (from the Old English).
Gleawecestre:	Gloucester.
Kingston upon Thames:	The first surviving record of Kingston is from 838 as the site of a meeting between King Egbert of Wessex and Ceolnoth, Archbishop of Canterbury. Kingston lay on the boundary between the ancient kingdoms of Wessex and Mercia, until in the early tenth century when King Athelstan united both to create the kingdom of England. Contrary to common belief the town has nothing to do with the King's Stone, the original meaning was 'the Kings Tun,' or a town with estates belonging to the king.

It is possible that the stone was taken from Stonehenge and conveyed to Kingston or from the local chapel at St Mary's: in both cases the stone was used as a mounting block.

Leofa:

"A thief named Leofa, whom King Edmund had banished for his robberies, returned after six years, and on the festival of St Augustine, archbishop of Canterbury, at Pucklechurch, unexpectedly took his seat among the royal guests. It was the day when the English were accustomed to hold a festival dinner in memory of him who had preached the Gospel to them, and as it happened he was sitting next to the thegn whom the king had condescended to make his guest at dinner. The king alone noticed this, for all the rest were aflame with wine; and in sudden anger, carried away by fate; he leapt up from the table, seized him by the hair, and flung him to the ground. The man drew a

dagger in stealth from its sheaf,
and as the king lay on him
plunged it with opening for
rumours about his death that
spread all over England. The
robber too, as the servants soon
came running up, was torn limb
from limb, but not before he had
wounded several of them."

Above account by William of
Malmesbury.

Housecarl's:	From the Old Norse - (*húskarl*, Old English - *huscarl*) was a non-servile manservant or household bodyguard in medieval Northern Europe.
Wilsætan:	The County of Wiltshire.
Wer:	In Anglo-Saxon and Germanic law, the wer was a price set upon a person's life on the basis of rank and paid as compensation by the family of a slayer to the kindred or lord of a slain person to free the culprit of

	further punishment or obligation and to prevent a blood feud.
Flyma:	An Anglo-Saxon word meaning - outlaw. Still used in North America to this day.
Gemot:	In Anglo-Saxon England a legal or administrative assembly of a community, such as a shire or a hundred.
Oferhyrnes:	Contemptible and disobedient.
Manung:	Following a reminder, the individual is deemed to be in default.
Hynden:	From the Old Norse meaning a comfortable person.
Bytt-fylling:	The filling of butts; an obscure expression referring to the festivities common at councils or local assemblies of the Anglo-Saxons, especially guild meetings.
Twy-Hynden:	Having a wergeld of two-hundred shillings.

Wergeld:	Money paid to the relatives of a murder victim in compensation for loss and to prevent a blood feud.
Hlaford:	A man of high rank in a feudal society or in one that retains feudal forms and institutions, especially the King, a territorial magnate or a proprietor of a manor.
Theow-men:	A slave.
Esne-workmen:	A servant.
Ēostre:	Easter

Alfred's Health

Alfred (Old English-Aelfred) was the fifth and youngest son of Ethelwulf of Wessex. He was born at Wantage sometime between 847 and 849, which lay at the foot of the Berkshire Downs, but now long vanished. It is a well-known fact that ill health marred Alfred's childhood.

The scribe, Asser, records him as being loved by his parents and brothers, and above all by his people.

Could it be possible that Alfred's medical condition may have unwittingly been the trigger that brought about the demise of the House of Wessex? Why were there so many early deaths within his family? What we do know is that Alfred suffered for most of his life with a Crohn's like medical problem for many years; therefore it is not unreasonable to wonder about the House of Wessex's fall. After all, Queen Victoria and haemophilia inadvertently brought about unrest in Europe and Russia.

Crohn's disease is often inherited, and one in five of its sufferers have a close relative with the disease or certainly ulcerative colitis. While the disease can affect people of all ages, it is primarily an illness of the young. It typically begins between the ages of fifteen and forty. No one knows for sure what triggers the initial intestinal inflammation, however at the start of the disease a viral or bacterial infection activates the immune system in the intestine.

King Alfred, was a known sufferer of inflammation of the intestines, was fifty years old when he died, as was his son Edward. Æthelstan was no more than forty-six and Edmund was only twenty-five, although we have no idea if he had a medical problem, having been assassinated. Eadred suffered from a longstanding illness which prevented him from consuming anything but the juices of his food, and he died at the age of thirty-two. Ælfweard died a mere sixteen days after his accession to the throne aged just twenty-two, and finally Eadwig only reigned for four years before his premature death aged nineteen years. No mention of an illness was recorded.

At present there is no cure for Crohn's disease, but medical treatment can control or reduce the symptoms and help stop them coming back. In Alfred's time no treatment existed.

King Alfred

𝕹ote from 𝕮harles 𝕯ickens

Æthelstan was lauded as a strong military leader, a scholar, and a devout ruler, yet by the Victorian era his reputation had so far been overshadowed by Alfred that Charles Dickens gave him one short paragraph in his 'Child's History of England'. Athelstan is one of England's greatest rulers yet remains very much a 'forgotten man'.

Sadly I am forced to agree with the sentiments of Mr Dickens.

Æthelflæd, the lady of the Mercia,
with her young nephew and future king - Æthelstan.

202

The Saxon dynasty died out when William Bastard of Normandy defeated King Harold Godwinson at the battle of Hastings. William was the illegitimate son of Robert I, duke of Normandy, by his concubine Arlette, a tanner's daughter from the town of Falaise. The duke, who had no other sons, designated William his heir, and with his death in 1035 William became Duke of Normandy at age seven. Rebellions were epidemic during the early years of his reign, and on several occasions the young duke narrowly escaped death. Many of his advisers did not. By the time he was twenty, William had become an able ruler and was backed by King Henry I of France. Henry later turned against him, but William survived the opposition and in 1063 expanded the borders of his duchy into the region of Maine.

In 1051, William is believed to have visited England and met with his cousin Edward the Confessor, the childless English king. According to Norman historians, Edward promised to make William his heir. On his deathbed, however, Edward granted the kingdom to Harold Godwinson, head of the leading noble family in England and more powerful than the king himself.

In January 1066, King Edward died, and Harold Godwinson was proclaimed King Harold II of England. William immediately disputed his claim. In addition, King Harald III Hardraade of Norway had designs on England, as did Tostig, brother of Harold. King Harold rallied his forces for an expected invasion by William, but Tostig launched a series of raids instead, forcing the king to leave the English Channel unprotected. In September, Tostig joined forces with King Harald III and invaded England from Scotland. On September 25, Harold met them at Stamford Bridge and defeated and killed them both. Three days later, William landed in England at Pevensey.

With only 7,000 troops and cavalry, William seized Pevensey and marched to Hastings, where he paused to organize his forces. On the thirteenth of October 1066, Harold arrived near Hastings with his army, and the next day William led his forces out to give battle. At the end of a bloody, all-day battle, King Harold II was killed–shot in the eye with an arrow, according to legend–and his forces were defeated.

The rest, as they say, is history.

But remember history is always written by the victor. Whatever William, the Duke of Normandy wanted to erase from Saxon history was removed. The only name he failed to completely obliterate was that of King Alfred, sadly Æthelstan, the first king of Britain, became the forgotten man and the forgotten king.

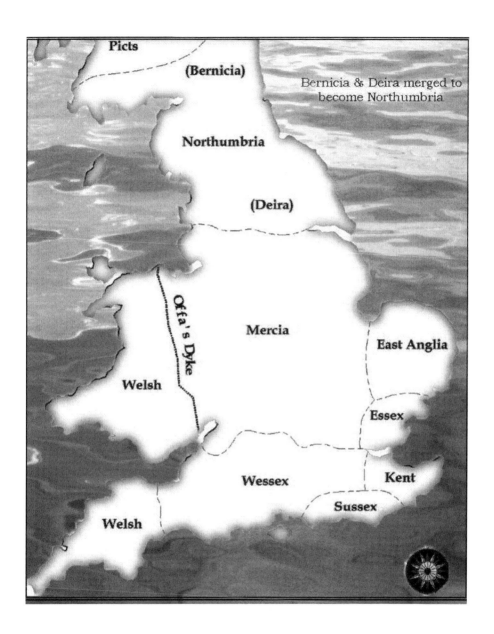

Picts

(Bernicia)

Bernicia & Deira merged to
become Northumbria

Northumbria

(Deira)

Offa's Dyke

Mercia

East Anglia

Welsh

Essex

Wessex

Kent

Sussex

Welsh

Æthelstan, the first king of England,
The forgotten man and sadly the forgotten king.

Notes

Printed in Poland
by Amazon Fulfillment
Poland Sp. z o.o., Wrocław

54653130R00116